NARROW ESCAPE

VANISHING RANCH
BOOK 9

CHRISTY BARRITT

CHAPTER
ONE

NATALIE WHITEHURST HEARD a noise and shot up in bed.

She glanced at her clock. It was barely past midnight.

Everything should be quiet at this hour. Her crew knew better than to wake her up.

Wasting no time, her feet hit the floor, and she tugged on a thick sweatshirt before grabbing her phone and her gun. She pulled on her work boots as she rushed toward her camper door.

Gripping her Sig, she threw the door open.

The inky black desert greeted her.

She thought she'd be used to this barren wilderness by now, but she wasn't.

The darkness felt piercing, to say the least.

She climbed down the three metal steps from her

trailer, stepped onto the dusty ground, and peered around. Cold late January air surrounded her, and she repressed a shiver.

No signs of movement caught her eye.

In front of her stood the partially built lodge she'd been charged with constructing for Vanishing Ranch. The project had broken ground two months ago, so they were just getting started.

She flipped on the flashlight atop her gun and shone the beam around her. "Hello?"

She hoped the sound had just been one of her workers. She had twenty men on her crew, and they were all living onsite in either modular homes or campers during construction.

Her boss had set up the lodging so the guys didn't have to travel back and forth more than thirty minutes each day. Everyone on her team lived in the Tucson area, not out here in the desert of western Arizona.

Maybe one of them had a little too much to drink and wandered outside his camper.

In Natalie's time working here, that hadn't happened yet. But that didn't mean it couldn't.

She paused and continued listening.

No other sounds filled the night.

But she hadn't imagined the noise.

Something had clanked, followed by a thump then a shuffle.

She took another step forward, her muscles still on edge.

She'd been in the military. Had gone into war zones. She knew how to handle herself in turbulent situations.

But that didn't mean she wanted any trouble out here.

She'd taken this job precisely to get away from any turmoil. But, in truth, her turmoil was all inside her—and it was hard to escape from that.

The noise sounded again.

Almost as if something had fallen over.

In the lodge.

What if vandals had come out here? Someone had left some graffiti on their work trailer a couple of weeks ago. If the troublemakers came back again, Natalie wanted to catch them red-handed.

By the time she called the county sheriff, whoever was inside could be long gone.

Natalie didn't want to wake up Charlie Soldier, her boss at Vanishing Ranch—and not just because the horse sanctuary was a mile away. Natalie had been entrusted with this job, and she tried to hold her own out here. She would call Charlie if it was an absolute emergency.

She walked toward the lodge and crossed the concrete at the front of the building.

The slab had been poured, the plumbing roughed in, and the framing was done. Just last week, they'd begun to plywood the walls and roof. This week they were working on some sheathing.

So far, they were making excellent time. But they still had a lot more work to do before this place was finished.

As she opened the door and stepped inside, the familiar scents of sawdust from freshly cut wood and gas from some of the equipment onsite surrounded her.

Darkness as thick as the desert soil closed in around her.

She realized she'd lowered her gun and jerked it back up.

The beam of her flashlight shone through the room, illuminating small dust and dirt particles in the air.

Though she could only see a few feet in front of her, she knew an unfinished, high-ceiling lobby stood before her.

And possibly an intruder.

"Who's in here?" Natalie tried to sound strong, but she heard the strain in her voice.

She was rattled. She knew how quickly things could go south.

As she waited for a response, she rubbed the small tattoo on her ring finger with her thumb and lifted a silent prayer.

But there was no reply.

A few seconds later, a new noise sounded from the west wing. A soft thud.

Almost like a muffled footstep.

Still gripping the gun, Natalie skirted some of the expensive equipment that had been left out—valuable equipment that could be stolen if vandals got brave.

She paced toward the sound, ready to act if she needed to.

Surely, whoever was inside had heard her call out. They wouldn't be taken by surprise.

But would she?

Her throat tightened at the thought.

She crossed the lobby and stepped toward the hallway, toward the wing of guest rooms. As she reached the first doorway, she cautiously turned toward it.

She scanned the unfinished space. It was roughly the size of a moderate hotel room, complete with its own bathroom. When the project was finished, the room would be fantastic.

As she shined her light on the plywood walls and wires dangling from the ceiling, a shuffling sounded behind her.

The next moment, someone tackled her. Pain ripped through her as her body collided with the wall.

As her gun flew from her hand, her head began to spin.

She had no time to compose herself before the shadow lunged at her again.

————

Joshua Madden hadn't been able to sleep.

He'd been sitting outside his trailer in a camping chair, drinking a bottle of water and watching the dark desert, when he'd heard something.

He figured it was his boss, Natalie Whitehurst, checking the work at the lodge.

He'd been watching her since he'd arrived five days ago and knew the woman was a perfectionist. She often liked to inspect the worksite after hours to make sure all the construction tasks had been done correctly.

No one else on the crew did that.

In fact, most of the crew did the minimum expected of them and then returned to their trailers for the evening to relax and enjoy themselves. The nearest town was too far away to visit after hours, although the other guys did try to make trips on the weekends when they could.

Doing construction work out in the desert wasn't easy or ideal, but the pay was good.

That's why most of the crew had signed on.

But not Joshua.

No one could know his real reason for taking this job.

Not if he wanted to survive.

His muscles tightened at the thought.

He heard another noise and glanced toward the sound. Natalie opened the door to her camper and turned on a flashlight.

Wait . . . if she was just leaving her camper now, then what had that noise been?

He stiffened, trying not to jump the gun.

Instead, he watched Natalie a moment.

Beautiful Natalie with her honey blonde hair, smattering of freckles, and slim figure. If he had to guess, she was in her early thirties. At first glance she looked more like the type who might want to work an administrative job, yet she was out here.

Although she held her own, he'd still been shocked she was the general contractor on this project. Not that women couldn't do these types of jobs. Not at all.

But usually, they chose other professions.

Natalie seemed tough but kind. Most of the guys on the crew respected her—although Joshua suspected that, at first, they'd probably had their doubts. However, from what he had observed so far, Natalie had earned their regard.

Joshua took another sip of his water, and his muscles tightened as he watched Natalie walking toward the lodge. Something about her tense, hunched stance sent up alarms.

This wasn't just an inspection or a secret meeting, was it?

She thought something was wrong.

Joshua stood. He'd planned to keep his distance and stay out of trouble, but he couldn't ignore the bad feeling in his gut.

Although Natalie seemed capable of handling herself, he didn't like the idea of a woman facing danger alone.

He flipped on the flashlight on his phone and walked toward the lodge.

Just as he reached the front door, he heard shuffling inside. Then a shout.

A crash cut through the air.

Heavy footsteps echoed in the barren space.

Wasting no more time, Joshua darted inside and shone his flashlight around.

He didn't see anyone in the lobby.

So where were those noises coming from?

As he heard a moan, he sprinted toward the sound.

He stopped in his tracks when he spotted two people wrestling in the hallway.

They slammed into the wall, backed up, and hit the other side.

Though it was dark and hard to make out anyone's features, one of them was taller than the other. Bulkier.

One man. One woman.

"Get away from me!"

Joshua recognized Natalie's voice.

The next instant, the man backhanded her.

Instincts kicked in, and Joshua dropped his phone as he lunged toward them. "What do you think you're doing?"

The assailant froze—but only temporarily.

Then the man shoved Natalie toward Joshua.

She slammed into him, nearly knocking Joshua off his feet.

The intruder darted in the opposite direction.

Joshua gripped Natalie's arm as he stared at her through the darkness. "Are you okay?"

She touched her bloody lip before nodding. "I'm . . . fine."

"Then I'll be back."

"Joshua, no . . . you don't have to." Concern laced her voice.

He barely heard her.

Instead, he sprinted after the man.

But the guy had a head start.

By the time Joshua reached the back of the lodge and rushed outside, the man had jumped onto a motorized dirt bike. Seconds later, the bike's buzz filled the air as the vehicle zoomed into the darkness.

Joshua stared after the intruder, knowing there was no way he could catch the guy now.

Just who had that man been? What was he doing inside the lodge?

If someone had come to steal equipment or tools, they would've needed to bring a vehicle to transport them, not a motorcycle.

Joshua didn't like the possible implications of this, and he prayed that tonight's intruder hadn't been trying to find . . . him.

CHAPTER TWO

NATALIE PULLED her hand from her lip. Even in the dark, she knew blood stained her fingers. She quickly wiped her hand on her black sweatpants.

That man had *definitely* caught her by surprise.

She frowned. She'd thought she was better prepared. Her husband had taught her everything she needed to know to succeed as a woman in this business.

Maybe she was losing her touch.

She stood, found a construction light, and flipped it on.

Brightness flooded the space.

The empty room around her stared back.

It appeared the same as it had earlier.

A table saw was set up in the corner. Various tools

were against the wall nearby. Someone's disposable coffee cup had been left forgotten on a worktable.

There was no indication an intruder had actually been there.

But he had.

She shivered at the thought of his large frame towering over her. Of his strong grip. His powerful hits. His tobacco-seared breath.

Then Joshua had intervened.

Thankfully.

As she gathered herself, her thoughts turned to Joshua.

The man had come to work for her just five days ago. He had a decent résumé and seemed pleasant enough. Plus, he didn't seem prone to drinking like some other crewmembers did. Though what they did in their off hours couldn't be dictated, drinking on the job was unacceptable—alcohol and construction work never mixed well.

Not that it mattered for the job, but Joshua was also nice to look at with his wavy blond hair and fit physique. Natalie had noticed from the moment she'd interviewed him that he had an easygoing demeanor but was like steel beneath that exterior—a fact that fascinated her.

She also hadn't been able to ignore how he always held the door for her. How he stayed later than the other guys to help her clean up. How he'd gained instant respect from the other crewmembers.

She was impressed.

Her husband had been all steel—inside and out, someone that people didn't mess with and who commanded respect wherever he went.

But when just the two of them had been together, he'd been gentle and sweet, showing another side of himself. A tender side.

But he wasn't here now, and he never would be.

Her heart panged at the thought.

A loud roar sounded outside, and her lungs tightened.

Where was Joshua? What if he'd been hurt?

Natalie should have insisted that he not chase that guy. She should've been more adamant.

But she hadn't expected him to take off as he did.

She hoped he was okay. That the roar she'd heard didn't indicate more problems.

It almost sounded like . . . a motorcycle. But what sense would that make?

Just then, a figure appeared at the end of the shadowed hallway, beyond the reach of the construction light.

Was it Joshua?

Or was it the man who'd attacked her?

She braced herself, reaching for her gun in her pocket.

But her weapon was gone.

That's right. When the man had attacked her, her Sig had flown from her grasp.

Panic rippled through her.

Where had it landed?

Natalie searched the floor but didn't see it.

She glanced up again as the man stalked toward her.

Should she run? Shout for help?

Instead, she backed toward the lobby.

"It's just me," Joshua's voice sounded. "It's okay."

The air left her lungs.

Her attacker wasn't here.

She could still feel where his fingers had dug into her arm.

But as Joshua came into view, Natalie saw the scowl on his face.

"Are you okay?" Natalie's gaze swept over him, but she didn't see any visible injuries—only his five o'clock shadow, dusty jeans, black T-shirt, and the loafers on his feet.

He shook his head, tension still stretched across his handsome face. "No, he got away. He had a dirt bike stashed near the door."

"But we didn't hear him approaching . . ."

"I suspect he rode his bike as close as he dared and then pushed it the rest of the way across the desert so he wouldn't alert us. When he fled, he no longer cared if anyone heard."

"No, I suppose it didn't matter at that point."

Joshua stared at Natalie's face and winced. "He got you good, didn't he?"

The man had managed to hit her more than once. Natalie touched her busted lip, then her swollen eye. But she shrugged, determined not to show any weakness. "I'll be okay. My pride is a little bruised, but otherwise I'm fine."

Joshua stared at her another moment before nodding and stepping back. He grabbed his phone from the floor and turned off the light before looking at her again.

"Any idea who that man was?" he asked.

"No." She glanced around. "I haven't had a chance yet to investigate and see what he may have been doing here. Nothing seems to be missing from what I can see, and my gut tells me he wasn't a squatter trying to find a place to sleep for the night. He was dressed in all black, and he seemed like he knew what he was doing, like he'd come here for a purpose."

"I have no doubt he was up to no good." Joshua shifted as he scanned their surroundings again before looking back at her. "Has this happened before?"

She shrugged. "A couple of weeks ago, I caught some guys out here tagging the place. When I yelled, they ran off. I haven't seen them since. But those guys seemed young, more the type to be into mischief than violence."

Joshua nodded down the hallway. "I don't mind checking the place out for you."

"How about we do it together?" Natalie wanted to see for herself what was going on. As far as she was concerned, this was her lodge. If you messed with it, you messed with her.

She finally spotted her gun on the floor several feet away and grabbed it, shoving the weapon into the front pocket of her sweatshirt.

After the man had knocked her gun away, he'd tossed her into the hallway, and it had been hand-to-hand combat. Natalie had tapped into a few of the skills she'd learned as a Navy officer—skills she'd thought she'd never use again.

She'd managed a few good punches, and the man had seemed surprised at first. But he quickly adjusted and came after her with more brute force.

She shuddered at the memory.

If Joshua hadn't shown up when he did . . .

She didn't even want to think about what could have happened.

Composing herself, Natalie stepped into the room she'd been searching when the man grabbed her. She glanced around again. She resisted another shiver when she remembered sensing the man's presence behind her.

He had taken her by surprise too easily.

Make sure you have eyes everywhere.

That's what Keith used to say.

Then she'd say, "That's impossible."

Still, she knew what he meant. She needed to be vigilant, aware of everything around her.

Joshua lingered in the doorway. "I was working in this room earlier. I don't see anything that appears missing or damaged."

Natalie shook her head, her cheek twitching as she fought a frown. "I don't either. But I have a feeling there's more to the story. Maybe this guy was looking for something."

"I'm not sure what he'd be looking for here. I suppose copper wiring is always a target for thieves. But not in this room."

Joshua had a point.

"I can check the entire lodge out more thoroughly in the morning," Natalie said. "Right now, it's too dark and it's late. We know this guy is gone so I suppose we should get some rest."

"Whatever you want, boss." His voice tightened ever so slightly.

Natalie stared at the man, wondering if his words were sincere or if he was going to go all macho on her, give her unsolicited advice, and insist he knew best because he was a guy.

She wasn't a feminist, not by any means. But she'd had enough conversations like this with men that she sometimes bristled defensively, even when the reaction wasn't warranted.

She turned toward him and nodded, careful to retain her professional demeanor. "Thank you for your help tonight."

He glanced at her busted lip again and frowned. "Do you have a first aid kit in your camper?"

Natalie nodded. For a moment, she imagined what it might be like if Joshua helped clean her wounds. What his tender touch might feel like. Pictured what it would be like to have someone take care of her for a change.

The thought sent a rush of warmth through her.

Warmth that she couldn't allow to seep in. She'd loved and lost before. She didn't want to go through that again.

She shoved her thoughts about Joshua aside as

she scolded herself. His assistance and/or care wouldn't be appropriate.

Besides, she could clean her wounds just fine by herself.

She'd been on her own since Keith, her husband, had passed away from stomach cancer four years ago. They'd only been married two years before he'd died. Their time together had been sweet, but entirely too short.

She cleared her throat. "I'll be fine. I doubt this guy will come back tonight, but both of us should remain vigilant. If you hear or see anything else, you know where to find me."

"Of course." Joshua's gaze remained on her, almost as if he could see through her words and bravado. As if he knew she was shaken and lonely—two things she rarely, if ever, admitted. Even to herself.

Why did she feel as if he could read her so well? It didn't make sense.

The realization left her feeling unbalanced.

Natalie stepped back. "Very well then. Good night, Joshua."

"Good night," he said, his voice deep and gravelly.

She knew without a doubt she needed to put more distance between herself and her newest hire.

She didn't like blurry lines.

Not at all.

Natalie was usually so careful about remaining professional.

She had to be, working around so many men.

In actuality, she hadn't done anything inappropriate. But her thoughts wanted to wander to places they shouldn't.

Places where she imagined what this man smelled like up close. What his story was. What it would be like to feel his hands at her waist. At the small of her back.

What his lips . . .

Nope. She knew that when temptation arose, there was only one thing to do.

That was flee, just like Joseph had run from Potiphar's wife.

Which was exactly why she hurried back to her camper and locked her door.

———

Joshua had done his research before coming here to Vanishing Ranch.

What he could find, anyway.

The information online was sparse, leaving

murky areas, things he didn't understand about this place.

There was an email listed as a contact method but no physical address.

No staff photos. Just pictures of horses.

They claimed the ranch was a horse rescue. That much was obvious. There was no doubt about that. Joshua had seen the stables and the horses being transported.

But there was also a steady influx of women and children coming to and from the property. Some were timid. Some sported bruises. Very few carried any luggage or bags with them.

Which made Joshua wonder if this place was involved with some type of human smuggling operation.

In which case, he wanted to know what was going on.

He'd taken almost daily walks toward the ranch compound. Early in the morning before work. Late in the evening.

He still hadn't seen her.

However, the ranch staff didn't let him beyond the gates. The woman running the ranch, Charlie Soldier, kept a tight rein on her operations. She made certain everyone working on the lodge stayed in their lane.

They claimed this place would be some type of desert getaway/dude ranch.

He glanced at the sprawling building, one featuring forty-eight rooms.

That *could* be true. The desert was a desirable destination for many, especially if those rescued horses could be used for trail rides.

But something about this seemed off.

Joshua needed to figure out what.

He stared at Natalie as she walked away, her trim figure disappearing into the night.

Six years as a Navy officer, and not a blemish on her record.

Her dad had been military, and so had her brother. She carried herself like a well-trained soldier, with her head raised and her shoulders squared. And she ran this operation like someone might run a ship. She had schedules and expectations, and she stuck to them.

She'd also been married for a couple of years to a man named Keith, who'd owned this construction business.

Yes, Joshua knew some personal details about Natalie.

He knew Keith had died four years ago. Natalie had a ring tattoo on her finger with a cross in the center. He wondered if that had been her wedding band.

Either way, Joshua was fascinated.

Not that he could let himself be fascinated. He'd come here for specific reasons and getting to know Natalie was not one of them. His motives were more life or death.

He watched as Natalie slipped back into her camper.

He then turned to study the horizon, looking for any glimmer of lights.

Listening for any out of place noises.

But the person who'd been here was now long gone.

Maybe this was the perfect chance for Joshua to take a better look around.

He turned on the flashlight on his phone and began his search in the lobby before moving into the kitchen.

Nothing.

He continued to the west wing.

Again, nothing.

As soon as he reached what would one day be the office area off the lobby, he paused. A strong scent of fuel permeated the area.

He shone his light on something in the corner, and his breath caught.

Gasoline cans. Lots of them.

The intruder had planned on burning this place down, hadn't he?

If Natalie hadn't walked in when she did, the man might have succeeded.

But how had he brought in all these cans on a dirt bike?

He couldn't have.

Joshua's muscles tightened.

What exactly was going on here?

AFTER NATALIE LEFT THE LODGE, she went to her camper and paused by her laminated pink kitchen counter as she considered her next options.

She'd come here for a simpler life. But why did it seem like a simple life just wasn't possible?

She leaned a hand against her desk as she collected her thoughts. Her split lip throbbed, as did her swollen eye and her head. Her pulse also pounded faster than usual.

Or maybe not.

Someone *had* just been trespassing on her construction site.

People didn't just *happen* to wander across this place. Vanishing Ranch was too far out of the way. If someone had come here, it was for a purpose.

But what?

And why was there something behind Joshua's eyes that seemed to indicate he knew more than he let on?

Or was Natalie just suspicious of everybody?

When she'd come here, she'd vowed to let down some of her walls. To give people a chance.

But maybe she was too closed off to do that. Losing her husband had turned her life upside down, and she still wasn't sure she'd come up for air yet. Keeping people at a distance seemed much safer than letting people in—safer for her heart, at least.

Suddenly, a knock rattled her camper door.

She jumped, her heartrate instantly kicking into double time.

She grabbed her gun and stared at the door, anticipating the worst.

Then she heard, "Natalie. It's me. Joshua. I found something you need to see."

She released her breath and placed her gun back on the table.

What else happened? What could he have found?

She'd thought the man had gone to bed.

Natalie opened the door, and the small light outside her camper illuminated his figure. She stared at him in his dusty jeans and faded black T-shirt.

It appeared he hadn't returned to his camper.

"What's going on?" she asked.

Joshua nodded toward the construction site. "I just walked through the lodge on my way back to my camper. I found something you're going to want to see."

Wordlessly, she stepped from her camper and followed Joshua into the lodge. He kept walking until he reached the office area. He then shone his flashlight in the corner.

Natalie sucked in a breath.

Gasoline cans had been tossed there. That was the sound she'd heard, the one that had awoken her. It had to be. Her camper was located closest to this end of the building.

"Was this guy going to burn the lodge down?" She hadn't realized she'd voiced the question aloud.

"He was probably bringing in all the supplies when you found him. If you'd been a few seconds later, he might have spread this gasoline, lit a match, and this whole place would be up in flames."

Natalie's chest tightened. She didn't like the sound of that.

"Why would anyone want to burn this place down?" she murmured.

"Maybe someone doesn't want the lodge to open."

"I suppose that's possible."

"But why would that be?" Joshua studied her

face. "Are you sure you haven't had any other trouble out here?"

Natalie bristled.

Maybe this man was too intelligent for his own good. Then again, the question was logical considering what had just happened.

She let out a long breath. "Nothing like this. Anyway, I need to call Charlie. She won't want to wait until the morning to hear about this."

"Probably a good idea."

Natalie grabbed her cell phone from her pocket, sucked in a breath, and then dialed her boss's number.

———

Joshua would never admit it aloud, but he was looking forward to interacting with Charlie Soldier. He'd been looking for more opportunities to get into her good graces so he could find out more information.

He didn't know much about the woman, only that her father had been a football star who'd given up a lucrative NFL career in order to fight for the military. While stationed overseas, he'd been killed.

He'd become a legend to many people because of his ultimate sacrifice.

Joshua also suspected there was more to Charlie's story than she admitted.

An ATV appeared down the road several minutes later, dust flying behind it. The vehicle pulled to a stop, and Charlie and her right-hand man, Monroe Davis, stepped out.

Joshua observed Charlie a moment. The woman had a cool confidence about her that even the darkness outside couldn't conceal. Her hair was long and dark with a touch of blonde on the ends, her eyes big, and her olive complexion smooth.

Charlie was tough. It was clear that she wasn't someone to be messed with, but she still had a feminine way about her.

Joshua could respect that.

She and Monroe strode to Natalie, concerned expressions on their faces.

Joshua was thankful Natalie had asked him to stay around. She'd said Charlie and Monroe might want to speak with him as well. No doubt, they would.

"I hear we have trouble," Charlie started, casting a quick glance at both of them.

Natalie nodded toward the lodge. "Let me show you."

They all walked inside, and Natalie turned on a few lights.

She led the way toward the office area while explaining exactly what they'd discovered. Charlie and Monroe were mainly quiet, simply listening as Natalie talked.

When they entered the room, Charlie stared at the gasoline cans, her jaw tight. "I don't like the sight of this."

"I was concerned as well, and that's why I didn't wait until morning to call you." Natalie frowned as she turned toward Charlie.

"I'm glad the two of you heard something before any damage was done. That's the good news." Charlie glanced at Natalie and did a double take. "This person did that to your face?"

Natalie reached for her lip again. "He put up a good fight."

"More like Natalie put up a good fight," Joshua chimed in.

Charlie frowned. "You should have told me. I could've called in the doctor."

"No need. I'm fine. I don't want to be a bother."

"You'll never be a bother."

"I appreciate that," Natalie said. "Thankfully, we were able to scare this guy off. I have no idea who it was. I didn't even get a good look at his face."

Charlie's gaze went to Joshua, and he reminded himself to look casual. Charlie was astute, and he couldn't give any indications that he had ulterior motives for being here.

"Did you see anything else?" she asked.

He shook his head. "Just what Natalie told you."

"How did that guy get all those gasoline cans here on a motorized dirt bike?" Monroe asked.

"That's a good question," Joshua said. "It makes me wonder if he'd stashed them somewhere nearby earlier and retrieved them tonight. Hard to say for sure."

As Charlie studied him another moment, Joshua reminded himself not to squirm.

"Okay, when it's daylight we'll investigate more but, in the meantime, we need to have someone out here keeping watch," Charlie finally said.

"My thoughts exactly." Natalie offered an affirmative nod.

"I have some ranch hands already on night watch who can take shifts patrolling the area. I'll also set up cameras and a security system like the one I have at the ranch. Someone went to a lot of trouble to do this, and I need to make sure it doesn't happen again."

The fact that Vanishing Ranch had a security system in place made Joshua's suspicions rise.

He fought a frown.

He was determined to figure out what exactly was happening at that ranch.

And he wasn't going to let anything stop him.

Not Charlie.

Not her right-hand man, Monroe.

And not his beautiful boss, Natalie.

Because what if these people were somehow involved with his cousin's disappearance?

He'd come here to find answers.

And he wasn't leaving without them.

NATALIE WASN'T GOING to let anything happen at her worksite, even if that meant going without sleep.

Sure, Charlie had said she'd send some of her guys out here to take shifts. But Natalie was quite certain that wouldn't start until later.

That's why Natalie decided she would keep watch over this place tonight.

Walking around in the desert in the dark wasn't exactly ideal. There were all kinds of hazards she could run into if she wasn't careful.

But she'd keep her eyes open and remain alert for danger.

She'd committed two years of her life to building Legacy Lodge for Charlie. The building was coming along faster than she'd anticipated, so maybe it wouldn't take quite that long.

When this job was done, she'd look for her next contract, wherever that may take her. She figured being a nomad was easier than settling down and facing the reality of her life as a young widow.

Besides, being out here on this ranch was growing on her. She didn't think she'd like the desert as much as she did, but she found it to be quite peaceful.

As she paced around the place, her gaze went to Joshua's camper.

The lights were still on. Maybe he couldn't get to sleep either. Part of that could just be adrenaline after everything that happened. But Natalie sensed he might also be unofficially keeping guard over the site.

As she paced, her phone buzzed.

Who would be messaging her at this time of night? It was almost two a.m. Could something have happened to her mom and dad back in Missouri? They were both in their late sixties, and she worried about them.

She paused and pulled her phone out, noting the text message from an unknown number.

Unknown numbers were never a good sign.

She knew she probably shouldn't, but she clicked

on the message anyway. A video popped onto her screen.

A video?

Another sign that she probably shouldn't watch.

Yet her gaze was inexplicably drawn to it.

She sucked in a breath when she saw the images on the screen.

They were images of a man who looked a lot like Joshua—only . . . different. His hair was longer. Greasier. He was unshaven and wearing dirty clothes.

He was with a group of thugs inside a rundown building. It was dark in the video and hard to make out very many details. But he appeared to have hold of a blindfolded woman in front of him.

He led her down a hallway. As they walked past the camera, Natalie saw the binds at the woman's wrists.

Saw how the man walked.

Her breath caught.

Was that Joshua Madden?

She couldn't be sure, but the similarities were notable.

Or was it . . . Albright Jones?

The two looked similar.

Either way, what was this guy doing with the woman?

Natalie didn't know, but she was going to find out.

She needed to figure out how to handle this situation.

———

The next morning, Joshua grabbed a breakfast burrito from the spread the chef at Vanishing Ranch had brought. Every morning, breakfast and lunch were delivered for the crew to eat. Dinner was on their own.

After he finished eating and drinking his coffee, he joined the rest of the crew.

It was time to get to work.

He hadn't slept much last night, but he was accustomed to functioning on little rest.

It came with the territory.

He wasn't one to sit idle.

At least, he had his work today to keep him busy. But he couldn't help but notice that Natalie was keeping a close eye on him.

Why was that?

Perhaps everyone here was now a suspect?

All he knew was that he needed to keep a low profile.

But keeping a low profile was easier said than done.

"Jeff isn't feeling well this morning." Enrico, the project manager, appeared beside him.

The man was in his fifties and had a strong Hispanic accent. Joshua knew the guy was Natalie's next in command. Apparently, the two of them went way back. The man seemed trustworthy enough, and he wasn't prone to the shenanigans that some of the other guys were.

Some of the crew had taken to booby-trapping camper doors, putting plastic wrap over toilets, and just generally poking fun at one another whenever possible. Mostly, they were bored, with little to entertain themselves out here.

"I'm sorry he's not well," Joshua said.

"He was supposed to do the sheathing up there." Enrico nodded toward the unfinished wall of the lobby. "I'm going to need you to go up instead."

"Whatever you need."

The scaffolding stretched ten feet across the wall and climbed almost up to the ceiling.

"Let's get started then." Enrico walked to the scissor lift and pressed a button to bring it closer to Joshua.

Joshua pulled on his safety harness and double-checked it. It was secure.

Then he climbed the scaffolding nearly fifteen feet to the top. It would be nice to have this room finished. Doing so would bring them one step closer to completion—but they were still a long way away.

Just as Joshua reached for the first piece of sheathing, he felt the platform shift beneath him.

He braced himself as adrenaline surged through him.

Below him, Enrico yelled his name.

Then the platform shifted again.

Joshua had personally checked the framework twice before clocking out yesterday.

It should be completely safe.

The scaffolding groaned. Metal clanged.

The next instant, the entire structure collapsed and sent him toppling to the ground in a heap of metal and wood.

CHAPTER
FIVE

NATALIE HEARD the crash and rushed inside the lobby, anticipating the worst.

Her heartrate thrust into triple time when she saw the pile of scaffolding on the floor.

Several workers were already digging through the rubble.

"Was somebody on that when it collapsed?" she shouted as she rushed toward them.

"Joshua," Enrico said as he pulled aside some of the debris.

Natalie began pulling off boards and pipes. "How did this happen? Didn't somebody check it?"

Safety first. That was her motto. As it was on *every* construction site.

"I inspected it at the end of shift yesterday so it

would be set to go this morning." Enrico threw a scaffolding tube out of the way.

Natalie began praying furiously as she dug through the rubble.

"Joshua? Can you hear me?" Enrico called.

No answer.

Natalie called out, "Joshua!"

Still nothing.

Anxiety clawed at her.

"Call for an ambulance!" she shouted to Pierre, one of the workers.

She couldn't afford for any of her crew to get hurt —and not just for financial reasons. Her reputation was on the line. She wanted to run a safe operation, and she was already going against the grain by being a woman in this field.

There was less room for failure for a female.

An unsafe jobsite . . . that could seal her fate.

As she moved aside another board, Joshua's face appeared. "I've got him! He's over here."

Joshua's eyes were closed, and he wasn't moving.

Natalie subdued the panic that wanted to race through her.

"I called 911. They are on their way," Pierre said before shoving his phone back into his pocket. "They promised to send a helicopter out."

The hard part about living out here in the middle

of nowhere was that medical help was far away. Entirely too far away.

In the meantime, Natalie was careful not to move Joshua, afraid that his back or neck could be broken. Instead, she put her fingers to his throat.

He still had a pulse.

Relief washed through her, but it quickly disappeared.

She wasn't sure how much longer his pulse would continue.

"Get the rest of this debris off of him," she called to the guys around her. "Then we need to give him space. Chester, go outside so when the copter arrives, you can flag it down and let the crew know where we are. Enrico, I need you to call Charlie and tell her what's going on before she sees the copter coming."

The two men did as she asked.

As the rest of the guys scrambled to remove the debris on top of Joshua, Natalie quickly took inventory of him.

Blood dripped from his hairline, his pant leg had a small rip, and several cuts stretched on his arm. Otherwise, on the surface, he appeared okay.

She took Joshua's hand and murmured, "We're going to get you through this."

Her mind raced through that video she'd seen of him last night.

This was no time to focus on that.

Right now, Natalie needed to concentrate on making sure Joshua survived this accident.

Then she would worry about how this had happened in the first place.

Natalie sat in the hospital waiting room, passing time until she heard an update on Joshua.

The helicopter had delivered him to Las Vegas Medical Center. Natalie, Charlie, and Monroe had driven there and were now waiting for a report from the doctor.

Dread pooled in Natalie's stomach, and she prayed the man wasn't hurt too badly. He'd maintained a steady pulse, but he hadn't regained consciousness when she'd last seen him.

Charlie and Monroe stepped back into the room with some coffee and bags of food in hand. They handed a cup to her, along with a turkey wrap and chips, before sitting beside her.

"Nothing new?" Charlie asked.

Natalie shook her head as she pulled open the bag of chips. She was hungry. "Nothing."

She popped a salty crisp into her mouth.

"Not to talk about business in times like these, but

OSHA is going to be all over this." Charlie crossed her legs and took a sip of coffee.

Natalie nodded, her appetite waning. "I know. My guys always check their equipment before use. I'm not sure what happened."

Keith had taught her well, and she knew how to run a safe site.

He'd been seven years older and was not only experienced but respected in the construction world. He had high standards.

"I have a couple of my guys looking into it. I'm also going to need to pull in workers' compensation. None of this is ideal."

"I know. And I'm sorry if I've let you down."

Charlie turned toward her. "Natalie, I hired you because I believe in empowering women. I love the fact that you're a successful woman in a male-dominated career. You couldn't have anticipated any of this happening. Understand?"

Natalie nodded, even though guilt still nagged at her. "Yes, thank you for your understanding and support. I believe in the mission of what you're doing and, more than anything, I want to help."

"Of course."

Natalie shifted as more thoughts swirled in her mind. "Honestly, I can't help but wonder if the site was sabotaged."

Charlie frowned. "I wondered that myself."

"There was that guy last night who was going to burn the place down . . ."

"But why sabotage the scaffolding if he was going to destroy the place anyway?" Monroe asked.

The burly man was quiet but wise. When he spoke, he had something important to say. And the way he looked at Charlie . . . it was pure love and admiration. Natalie wasn't sure Charlie even realized it—or, if she did, if she returned his feelings.

"That's a good point. None of this is adding up."

"Natalie . . ." Charlie shifted toward her. "I hate to ask this, but I have to. Is there anyone in your life who might want to do this to you?"

"In my life?" She blinked with surprise at the question.

"I hate to ask, but I'm just trying to explore every option. I know your husband had some pretty powerful clients."

Yes, most of the men he'd worked with had been wealthy developers.

Natalie's thoughts wandered back to that video sent to her last night, the one where it looked as if Joshua was escorting a woman who'd been tied up. Should she mention it to Charlie?

She didn't know for sure it was Joshua in the video. The man could also pass for Albright Jones . . .

which didn't make any sense. Albright was a busi-nessman who'd hired her husband to build a resort for him. Keith had sensed the man had some nefar-ious plans for the place, and he'd backed out of the project. Threats had followed.

But Albright was wealthy and had people who did everything for him. It didn't make sense that he'd look like this.

Which brought her back to Joshua again.

If it *was* Joshua . . . someone *could* be trying to set him up. Otherwise, why would the sender have remained anonymous? And how had this person gotten her number? How had they known Joshua worked for her?

So much didn't make sense.

"Natalie?"

Charlie's voice brought her from her thoughts.

Natalie straightened and swallowed hard. "There was one man named Albright. He's a developer in the Phoenix area, and the business relationship between him and my husband, Keith, was very contentious."

"We'll look into him," Charlie said. "Anyone else?"

She drew in another deep breath. "I suppose there's Lou."

"Who's Lou?" Monroe asked.

She released the deep breath. "He *was* a member of my crew. A couple of weeks ago, we all went into town on a Sunday afternoon. I don't usually go with the guys, but there was a football game on, and I thought it might be good for the crew's morale. It started nice with wings and football. But . . ."

"What happened?" Charlie's eyes narrowed.

"Lou began hitting on me—aggressively. So much so that when I went to the bathroom, he followed me, pushed me up against the wall, and tried to kiss me."

"You didn't report that to us." Charlie's voice stiffened. "We could have helped."

Natalie shrugged. "I fired him. Told him to get his things and leave. He wasn't very happy, but I got Enrico and a couple of other guys to help. I wanted to handle it myself if I could. My husband used to always say, 'Don't rely on other people to do what you're capable of doing yourself.'"

Natalie stared at Charlie, and she wasn't sure if the woman was impressed or irritated at her decision. Finally, Charlie leaned back and nodded. "We'll look into him also. I'm sorry that happened to you. You haven't heard from him since then?"

"No, but he was muttering some threats when he left. I figured they were empty."

Just then, the doctor stepped into the room, and they

all straightened as they anticipated what he had to say. The fortysomething man pushed gold-framed glasses up higher on his thin nose, a tired look about him.

"He's going to be fine," the man announced. "He has a slight concussion and a bruised rib. But with a little rest, he should recover just fine."

The breath left Natalie's lungs. "That's good news."

"Of course, he won't be able to work on the jobsite for a while." The doctor glanced at Natalie. "But I'm assuming you already considered that possibility."

Natalie nodded. "Of course."

"Give us ten more minutes, and you can go in to see him."

After the doctor walked away, Charlie pressed something into Natalie's hand.

Natalie glanced at the key fob there.

"I had someone bring you a car," Charlie explained. "I have a meeting I can't miss at the ranch, but I didn't want to leave you here without a way to get back."

"Thank you."

"We'll deal with OSHA and workers' comp later. And, of course, we'll cover any of Joshua's bills for his hospital visit."

"I'll keep you informed on his condition," Natalie added.

After they left, she stared at the file in her purse. It contained the information Joshua had filled out when he'd taken this job.

She'd grabbed the folder before she left the jobsite.

Of course, she'd reviewed it before. But she hadn't been looking for anything out of the ordinary at the time.

She opened the file now and looked at the information. Joshua Madden was from South Carolina. Thirty-four years old. Single.

Emergency contact? None.

Health insurance? None.

She frowned.

It appeared there was no one Natalie could contact for him.

Still, something about his personal file felt off, incomplete.

When Joshua had given the paperwork to her initially, she'd questioned him about his lack of insurance. However, in her line of work, it wasn't that unusual for construction workers to switch companies often and allow medical benefits to lapse.

But the more she got to know Joshua, the more she thought there was something different about him. He seemed like the type to have all his "ducks in a row," as her grandmother used to say.

She frowned and glanced at her watch.

In five more minutes, maybe she would have some answers.

CHAPTER
SIX

JOSHUA PULLED HIS EYES OPEN, grogginess enveloping him.

He blinked several times before glancing around. He noted the blurry machines he was hooked up to. The dry erase board on the wall in front of him with words written on it.

He squinted. It appeared to be the date and the name "Nurse Tanya" scrawled with a black dry-erase marker.

A TV was mounted in the corner.

A curtain hung halfway around his bed.

He was in the hospital, he realized.

He moved his arm and felt the IV there. Took a breath and felt the cannula in his nose. Shifted his finger and felt the oxygen monitor.

Memories of being on the scaffolding hit him.

Memories of the platform shifting. Of the men around him yelling. And then of falling and hitting the ground, followed by scaffolding colliding with his body.

How had the safety harness failed? It didn't make sense.

The good news was that he was alive.

He took a quick assessment of his injuries. Saw a few scrapes and bruises on his arms. Felt the soreness on his side. A knot on his head.

Overall, he'd say things could be much worse.

He shoved his head back into his pillow and sighed.

He'd been drifting in and out of consciousness for . . . well, he wasn't sure how long.

But it wasn't a total shock he was here.

Now he needed the doctor to come in and give him an update.

He shifted, the motion instantly making him wince. His hand went to his side.

Yes, he was going to be in pain for a while.

He glanced out the window. He appeared to be on the second floor of the hospital.

What city was he in? Was anyone here with him?

The questions swam through his muddled mind.

A knock sounded at the door.

Before Joshua could call, "Come in," it opened, and Natalie stepped inside.

Something about seeing her brought him both a strange sense of comfort and a rush of nerves.

He wasn't usually the nervous type. He couldn't be in his line of work. One small tell, and his whole cover would be blown.

"Hey there." Natalie closed the door behind her. "I'm glad to see you're awake."

The sight of her was much welcome after what had happened.

As he shifted, he tried not to cringe again as pain rippled through his side. "Glad to be awake."

She placed her purse in an empty chair before pausing near the foot of his bed. "That was quite a scare you gave us."

"Tell me about it. I inspected that scaffolding and the harness myself the day before. They were fine. Don't know why my personal fall arrest system didn't work."

The look in her eyes seemed to indicate that she knew more.

Before he could ask, the doctor stepped into the room. Perfect timing.

"Well, you're one lucky man." The man paused beside Natalie. "We'd like to keep you here overnight just for observation. But overall, I'd say that you're doing well."

"Is staying here really necessary?" The last thing Joshua wanted was to waste time being here in the hospital. Something was going on at the jobsite, and he wanted to know what.

"As you can imagine, we have to take these things seriously."

Joshua wanted to argue more but decided not to. If he fussed too much, it would only raise suspicions, and that was the *last* thing he needed.

The doctor chatted a few more minutes before leaving.

Then a nurse came in and took his vitals.

He waited until she left before glancing back at Natalie, knowing his conversation with her would probably turn in an unwelcome direction.

"We have some things we need to discuss . . ." Natalie started, just as he'd expected.

His gaze wandered toward the window, and he sat up straighter.

In the distance, four men climbed from a car in the parking lot.

Four men Joshua recognized.

Four men who were here to look for him.

Four men who would kill him at first sight . . . and anyone who happened to be nearby.

The questions Natalie wanted to ask Joshua were poised on the tip of her lips.

She wasn't normally the timid type. But still, she needed to be careful about how she brought up the subject of that video she'd been sent.

She'd learned a lot about being a businesswoman as she'd gained more experience as a general contractor. She'd learned how to approach certain subjects carefully and with more than a little finesse.

Blurting her suspicions outright could put her in a bind.

She'd lose any advantage she might have.

Before she could start, Joshua threw his legs off the bed, seeming to get a second wind. "I need my clothes."

"Excuse me?" Her breath caught with surprise—and confusion. "You shouldn't be getting up."

Maybe Joshua's concussion had affected him more than she'd assumed.

"I don't have a choice." He glanced around, his expression pinched with discomfort. "Where are my clothes?"

Natalie pointed to a bag on a shelf near the bathroom. "I'm assuming they're over there."

"Get them for me. Please."

Before she could respond, he jerked out his IV. Blood gushed from the insertion point.

Natalie squeezed her eyes shut and looked away. She *hated* blood.

"What are you doing?" she muttered, feeling a panic-induced headache coming on.

Joshua was acting erratic. Maybe she should call the doctor back in here. Was this because of his head injury?

"I don't have time to explain. Just listen to me and get my clothes."

Natalie turned back toward him and crossed her arms, not liking his bossy tone. "I'm not the type who responds well to demands."

Joshua threw his oxygen cannula on the bed. "Believe me, you're going to want to listen to me right now. We have to get out of here."

He stood, taking only a moment to find his balance.

A new urgency stretched through each of his motions.

His gaze locked with hers. "If you don't get me my clothes, in less than two minutes four armed and dangerous men are going to come in this room and kill us both. So if you don't mind cooperating, I'd appreciate it."

His words echoed in her head.

Kill them?

She sucked in a breath.

Yes, there was definitely more to his story.

She had only a split second to decide how to react.

Natalie grabbed his clothes and tossed them to the bed. "Get moving."

"STAND WATCH AT THE DOOR," Joshua told Natalie.

"Stand watch?" She stared at him as if he were speaking a different language.

He decided to try a different approach as he grabbed his jeans and pointed to his hospital gown. "I need to change clothes. Some privacy would be nice."

Those words seemed to work.

Natalie turned and remained by the door.

"I need you to tell me if you see them coming."

"Okay." But she left it only open a crack. "What do these guys look like?"

"You'll know when you see them."

"And if I do see them . . ." Her voice cracked. "What are you going to do?"

"Did you bring your gun? I know you conceal carry."

She glanced back at him before quickly correcting her line of sight and looking back out the door.

But Joshua had seen her cheeks redden as she'd glanced at his chest when he pulled his blue work shirt on.

In different circumstances, he'd think it was flattering. Not now. Not with so much at stake.

"I'm not supposed to have a gun in the hospital," Natalie finally murmured.

"That's not what I asked. Did you bring it?" He buttoned up his shirt as quickly as possible, ignoring the sharp pain in his side. His clothes were covered in dust, and a small amount of blood stained his jeans. But they'd work for now. He had no other choice.

Even with Natalie's head turned toward the door, he saw the frown cross her features.

She nodded toward her bag, which she'd left on the spare chair near the window. "It's in my purse."

"You'd better grab it. We might need it." He ignored the ache in his ribs as he managed to slip his feet into his boots.

His condition right now certainly made it harder to escape. But he didn't have much choice.

Joshua grabbed her purse and then rushed to join her near the door. But as he reached her, Natalie backed inside, nearly bumping into him.

Fear raced through her gaze as she glanced at him. "It's them. They're coming this way."

Joshua's muscles tightened.

They were too late. They couldn't just walk out of here.

He needed to think of another way to escape. But the glass in these hospital windows was practically unbreakable and they were on the second floor. And there was only one door leading out of his room.

If he and Natalie stayed in here, they would be easy targets and definite victims.

And he couldn't let Natalie be injured . . . not because of him.

———

Natalie's thoughts raced.

As Joshua leaned into her, she was entirely too aware of how close he was. Aware of his body heat. Aware of the faint scent of sawdust on him—an aroma she'd always loved.

Those were *not* the things she wanted to be thinking about right now.

Instead, her thoughts went to the gun in her purse. She didn't want to use it. Especially not in a hospital.

She prayed it didn't come down to that.

But if this situation was as dangerous as Joshua had implied, then how would they get out of it?

Just then, a group of medical students rounded the corner and began pacing down the hallway toward them.

Joshua gripped her arm. "This is our opening. We need to move. Now."

Those men glanced in each room they passed, clearly looking for someone.

Knowing she had no time to argue, Natalie let Joshua lead her in front of the students.

She was concerned about his condition. His heavy breathing. How he limped and grasped his side.

Under any other circumstances she would refuse to help him leave.

She'd say there was another way out of this, but she had a feeling there wasn't. If they were going to get out of this situation alive, then they needed to flee now.

Natalie prayed that no one else got hurt in the process.

With the students behind them blocking the view

of those men, she and Joshua rushed toward the opposite end of the hallway.

They had to get away without being seen.

Their lives depended on it, and Natalie needed to survive long enough to find some answers.

JOSHUA FELT the tension in the air.

He and Natalie didn't have much time to get out of here.

Thankfully, he spotted an exit at the end of the hallway and headed that way.

The stairs would be agony on his ribs. But he had no other choice.

Just as he and Natalie reached the door, a shout sounded behind them. "Hey!"

Joshua looked over his shoulder and saw the four men rushing down the hallway toward them.

Forgetting his pain, Joshua pushed Natalie through the exit. "Move. Now!"

They dashed down the stairway. Thankfully, they were only on the second floor.

As soon as they reached the lobby, they rushed

toward another back exit—toward the parking lot. At least, if Joshua understood the hospital layout correctly, that's where it was.

"Do you have a car?" he asked Natalie.

"Charlie left me one."

"Where is it?"

She quickly shook her head, almost looking frazzled. "I have no idea. I didn't think I'd need to use it this soon."

As Joshua heard more footsteps thundering behind him, he knew they didn't have any time to contemplate this.

They needed to find that vehicle and get out of here.

How had Tomas Herrera's men even found him?

That's who they were. He was certain of it.

Were they the ones behind what had happened at the lodge?

Joshua would need to figure that out later.

Right now, he needed to come up with an escape plan.

———

Natalie stared at the cars in front of her, her heart beating rapidly against her chest.

She had no idea what make or model to look for.

Then a new sound split the air.

Gunfire.

Her breath caught.

Those guys were behind them, and they were moving in quickly.

Behind her, people screamed and ran.

Joshua's hand pressed into her back. "We've got to find that car."

Her hands trembled as she reached into her pocket and fished out the key fob Charlie had given her. She clicked the fob and held her breath, praying this would work.

A moment later, she heard a *beep* coming from an SUV in the second row.

She lifted a prayer of thanks.

The two of them raced toward the SUV. As Joshua headed toward the driver's side, Natalie nudged him out of the way.

"There's no way you're driving with all the pain medication you're on." She gave him a look. "Passenger seat. Now."

Joshua certainly had to know that him driving was a bad idea. He stared at her only a second before obliging.

They jumped into the vehicle, and Natalie cranked the engine. As another bullet cut through the air, she threw the SUV into Reverse. Quickly, she backed out and then jerked the gearshift into Drive.

She pressed the accelerator and charged toward the exit.

As she zoomed past the gate, she glanced in her rearview mirror in time to see the men pause behind them.

And she wished she was naive enough to think this was all over.

But she knew it was only a matter of time before those guys jumped into their own vehicle and followed them.

This ordeal was far from being over.

CHAPTER
NINE

JOSHUA GRIPPED HIS SIDE, ignoring the pain pulsing through him.

"There." He pointed to the street in front of them. "Go to the right."

Natalie didn't ask any questions. Instead, she jerked the wheel and headed away from the hospital.

Joshua needed to make sure no civilians were injured right now. He'd never forgive himself if someone got hurt.

He was about to yell another direction to Natalie when she turned to the right again.

Good. He knew the woman was capable and smart.

But very few people had been in situations where they needed to know how to handle themselves in a highspeed chase.

That was exactly what they were about to experience.

As they merged onto a larger, busier highway, Joshua glanced around.

Vegas. They were in Vegas, he realized.

He recognized the buildings in the distance.

He turned and looked behind them.

A black sedan swerved onto the highway.

It was them.

The men.

They'd caught up more quickly than Joshua had anticipated.

Just as before, he was about to shout an instruction. But as if reading his mind, Natalie turned before he could say anything.

As she did, the back window shattered. Natalie let out a scream.

These guys were shooting at them while on the busy, public road.

"Joshua . . ." she muttered.

"You're doing fine."

As Natalie swerved, Joshua's heart pounded harder.

How had these guys even found him at the hospital?

And an even bigger question—how were he and Natalie going to get away unscathed?

———

Natalie gripped the wheel so tightly that her knuckles hurt.

She still heard the sound of the bullets flying. Of the glass shattering.

These guys weren't playing.

One slipup, and she and Joshua would be dead.

She had to think of a way out of this. Otherwise, there would be a high-speed chase through Las Vegas traffic. One that would probably end with a crash. One that would put innocent people in the line of danger.

She couldn't live with herself if she hit someone.

She needed to figure out another plan.

"Any ideas on what to do?" she asked Joshua as if he would know.

But he did seem to know. In fact, he seemed rather skilled at escaping and evading.

Just for a moment, her mind flashed back to that video she'd been sent—a video possibly of Joshua.

If that was him, there was far more to this man than she'd initially realized.

Who exactly had she hired? Had she made a grave mistake?

Trouble seemed to be following them at every turn.

Or maybe—just maybe—this was connected to her.

What if Albright had sent those guys? Or if they were Lou's friends?

Yet Joshua seemed to recognize them instantly, which indicated he'd seen them before.

"I'm looking for a way out of this." Joshua glanced around, his body tense. "For now, keep changing directions. We need to make sure there's enough of a gap between our SUV and theirs so we can get away."

Again, he said the words as if he was an expert.

But those would be conversations for another time.

Natalie sped toward a traffic light, barely slowing as she turned left onto another side road.

Cars braked and squealed around them.

She held her breath, bracing herself for possible impact.

But it didn't come.

However, they weren't out of danger yet.

She glanced in her rearview mirror.

A moment later, the car appeared. Again.

There *was* a gap between them now, but she wasn't sure how long that space would remain.

As she glanced ahead, she spotted the answer she was looking for.

She held her breath, knowing this move would be tricky.

But she had no choice right now.

As she calculated the risk, she pressed the accelerator harder.

If she was even one second off in her timing, her plan would fail . . . and have fatal results.

CHAPTER
TEN

JOSHUA SUCKED in a breath when he saw the train charging along the tracks.

Heading straight toward the road in front of them.

"Natalie . . ." His breath caught.

She pressed the accelerator harder. "We don't have any other choice."

He gripped the armrest. "Natalie . . . we're not going to make it."

"Yes, we are."

His heart thrummed harder.

If they made it across those tracks, it would be a near miracle.

Apparently, that's what Natalie was counting on.

He'd feel better if he were behind the wheel.

She pressed the accelerator even harder, and they zoomed toward the oncoming train.

Joshua almost didn't want to watch.

The locomotive was mere seconds away from crossing the road.

The train whistle blew in warning.

The lights flashed on the railroad crossing sign.

The dinging sound warned them to stop.

But there were no cars in front of them preventing them from crossing. No arm swinging down to block them.

It was just the open road ahead.

If they got through, it would be by the skin of their teeth, as his dad used to say.

As they reached the tracks, Joshua glanced beside him.

The engine was mere yards away.

The train whistle screamed at them again.

If they were one second too late, they'd be smashed to smithereens.

———

Natalie held her breath and pressed the accelerator to the floor.

She could practically feel the heat coming from the train.

Could feel its powerful engine vibrating on the tracks beneath them.

They were *that* close.

Close enough to feel the tension that zoomed through the air.

Just as they reached the other side of the tracks, the locomotive charged past.

But her heart didn't slow. Not yet.

That had been too close.

Surprisingly, Joshua remained silent.

Part of her wanted to brake. To sit on the road a moment and get her anxiety under control.

But she couldn't afford to do that. Time was a luxury they didn't have.

Those guys were waiting on the other side of the train tracks.

She needed to use this time to her advantage and put space between them and those gunmen.

But death had been so close she could practically taste it.

"Smooth moves back there," Joshua finally muttered as they headed down the road through an industrial area.

"I don't know if those were smooth moves or God's grace. Maybe both."

Joshua studied her a minute as if analyzing her words.

"What?" she asked.

"You're a believer?"

"I am."

"I thought so."

"Why do you say that?" She turned onto another road, maintaining her speed.

He shrugged. "Just through observation. The way you close your eyes sometimes before speaking, almost as if praying. The cross tattoo on your finger that you touch when you're stressed. The kindness you show when it's undeserved."

She nearly stopped breathing. He'd noticed all those things? Was she that obvious?

Or was he that observant?

At the thought, she touched her tattoo—the one she'd gotten in lieu of a wedding ring. With her and Keith's jobs, a tattoo had just made more sense.

Natalie wanted to relax at Joshua's words.

She didn't.

Not when so much was at stake.

Finally, ten minutes later, she pulled between a barricade of parked cars in the lot outside a large department store.

Now that she'd lost those guys, she couldn't keep driving.

Her hands were still shaking.

She needed answers.

Natalie put the SUV in Park and turned to Joshua.

"You have some explaining to do."

CHAPTER
ELEVEN

JOSHUA BRACED himself for the coming conversation.

"I'm not going anywhere else until you start talking." Natalie crossed her arms, that confident, bossy look in her eyes.

Even though he'd known this interrogation was coming, he still didn't know exactly how he should answer. He couldn't be hasty right now.

She impatiently tapped her finger against her arm. "Well? And please don't tell me you're just some construction worker who just happens to know how to elude people in a car chase and, for that matter, has people pursuing you with guns."

"It's a long story," Joshua started, even though he knew his words sounded lame.

"I'm going to need more than that. I just put my

life at risk. Maybe even my career. If you are some kind of criminal and I just helped you escape, Charlie will fire us both. So you need to start talking."

Joshua let out a long breath and rubbed his hand over his jaw as he contemplated what to say.

Did he trust Natalie? Or was she in on whatever scheme was going on at Vanishing Ranch?

He didn't know.

However, he couldn't blow his cover. Yet, what other choice did he have at this moment? He needed Natalie on his side.

His temples pounded as he said, "You won't believe me if I tell you the truth."

"Try me. And I'm beginning to lose my patience. If that happens, I will kick you out right here and leave you on the side of the road while I head back to the ranch. After I call the police, that is. Do you understand?"

Well, when she put it like that . . .

He frowned and let out a long breath before admitting, "I'm looking for my cousin. Her name is Bella Rivers."

Natalie narrowed her eyes. "And you think you're going to find her out in the middle of the desert?"

"No. But I'm afraid something happened to her. I

believe she was at Vanishing Ranch at some point after she disappeared."

Some type of comprehension lit Natalie's gaze, and Joshua realized she knew more than she'd probably ever admit.

He waited, hoping she'd say something.

Finally, she asked, "When was the last time you talked to your cousin?"

"Two and a half months ago. I've been looking for her ever since."

"You two must be close."

"She is like a sister to me," Joshua said. "My own parents were killed in a car crash when I was thirteen. I went to live with my aunt and uncle—and Bella. She's five years younger than I am."

"I see."

"My aunt and uncle weren't great, though. My uncle has anger problems, and my aunt was too timid to say anything to him. I'm not saying they were abusive, but the house was dysfunctional, for sure. Then my uncle left us to live with some woman he'd met on a business trip. Bella was only fourteen when that happened. Afterward, she began making a string of bad decisions."

"That can be the pattern that happens at times."

"Of course, those bad decisions were mostly with guys. Not to sound like a psychologist or anything, but I feel like she was looking for the love she never felt from her father. She's had so many bad relationships. But Grundy was the worst."

"Who is that?"

"The guy she eventually married. He's a truck driver. Seemed charming at times, but I could see something simmering beneath his gaze. Three months into their marriage, she seemed like a different person, a shell of who she'd once been. I begged her to let me help her, but she wouldn't even admit anything was wrong."

"I'm so sorry. That must have been difficult. Then she disappeared?"

His jaw tightened. "That's right. I . . . I was working out of town without access to my phone. But when I had the chance, I tried to call her. It went right to voicemail. I called Grundy, and he claimed she'd left him. That's all he would say. But I sensed something in his voice—like he was hiding something."

"What's your theory?"

He let out a sigh. "I never trusted her husband. I'm afraid he did something to her. But he won't admit anything. He's even in jail now for an unrelated charge—disorderly conduct during a bar fight—and he still isn't fessing up to anything. I'm not going to give up until I find her."

"Where did you catch wind that she could be at Vanishing Ranch?" She narrowed her eyes as if trying to put the pieces together.

"That's another long story, one I'd rather not get into. But I promise you that looking for her is the only thing I've been up to while working at the lodge."

"I'd like to believe that, but . . . what about those gunmen following you?" Natalie's gaze latched onto his as she searched for the truth.

He swallowed hard. "I may have run into some trouble in the past."

"I checked your record," Natalie said. "I didn't see anything."

"Let's just say this trouble was off the books."

Joshua waited for her reaction, bracing himself for whatever transpired next.

He hoped—and prayed—that she'd bought his story . . . because it was the truth.

With a few important details left out.

———

Natalie's thoughts raced.

What if this was all just a cover story? What if Joshua was really the abuser, and he'd come here looking for his victim—not really his cousin—under the guise of trying to help her?

She'd seen it happen before. Men who were desperate to find the women they were abusing. Often, they would start searching and scouring the area, asking for help as if they were worried about a loved one. They would get the community involved by posting tearful pleas online. But, in fact, they were preying on the sympathies of others in order to continue their abuse and pattern of control.

If that was the case with Joshua, Natalie wasn't going to play any part in this.

However, if Joshua knew something about the ranch that he wasn't letting onto, she couldn't simply let him go and hope that he would leave them alone. Besides, that video . . . if that had been Joshua on that clip, then this very well could be some kind of well-orchestrated scheme.

No, she needed to bring Charlie into this. She should have brought her in earlier, for that matter. But as the saying went, hindsight was twenty-twenty.

Joshua already knew where the ranch was located, so it wasn't like she would be revealing anything if she took him back there.

In his current injured state, he might not be able to fight for a while. But it would be easy to take him down if he didn't have backup. And Natalie knew for a fact that he didn't have a gun on him. Hers was tucked into her purse, which was on the other side of her, where he couldn't reach it.

She sighed and scanned the parking lot for any signs of trouble before turning back to Joshua. "Do you have a picture of Bella?"

He nodded and cringed with pain as he reached into his back pocket for his phone.

No doubt any movement like that wouldn't feel good.

While he pulled up the picture, Natalie checked the parking lot one more time. But she didn't see anything suspicious.

Finally, he showed her an image of a woman in her early twenties with curly dark hair and a tentative smile.

Natalie didn't recognize her. Then again, she'd only been at the ranch three months, and she spent most of her time working on the lodge.

"Have you seen her before?" Joshua studied her face.

Natalie shook her head. "I'm sorry, I haven't."

He frowned. "We were so close growing up, and I almost didn't join the military because of her. I wasn't sure how she'd do if I was gone. Now, I wish I'd stayed."

"I can imagine how difficult this is for you." Natalie locked her gaze with his. "But I still need to know how you potentially tracked her to Vanishing Ranch. Don't tell me it's a long story. That's not going to cut it."

Joshua didn't seem offended by her statement. Instead, his gaze remained steady. "I've been following her trail. I met a man at the bus station in Kingman who said that he talked to her at a stop back in Winslow. He said some guy who worked at Vanishing Ranch picked her up. Said she looked scared. That's what brought me out this way."

Most of the women heading to Vanishing Ranch *did* look scared. They were literally running for their lives, and nothing was certain any longer.

But Bella hadn't been scared because of the man who'd picked her up.

The situation went far deeper than that.

But Natalie couldn't tell Joshua that.

"So now that you know why I'm really here, I want to talk to Charlie. If my cousin was ever at the ranch, she would know about it. Will you take me to see her?" Joshua stared at Natalie, his gaze unblinking as he waited for her response.

She stared out the window, searching for any more signs of trouble as her thoughts churned.

She didn't see anything.

But she needed to figure out what she would do next.

Because the fact was . . . trouble sat right here beside her in the SUV.

And she still wasn't sure if she trusted Joshua or not.

JOSHUA STARED at Natalie as he waited for her answer.

Will you take me to see her?

Such a simple question, but so much depended on her response.

He knew Natalie was intelligent.

But Joshua had no idea what she was thinking.

She could decide to fire him on the spot and leave him in this parking lot.

Or she could decide to help him out.

The only thing he knew for sure was that he needed Natalie on his side. This could be his only chance to find out what was going on at the ranch.

Too many secrets surrounded that place.

He needed to know what they were.

Finally, Natalie released a long breath and

nodded. "I'll take you back to the ranch. But Charlie needs to know what you just told me. All of it."

His throat constricted. "Of course."

"I'm not sure what Charlie will do. You came here under false pretenses. We take security at the ranch very seriously." Natalie held his gaze.

That was another thing that he found so strange. Why so much security for rescued horses?

Talking to Charlie was really the best option. She had the answers he needed. Joshua had been struggling to find a way to get his foot in the door with her.

Maybe this was it. But he was going to have to be very careful how he proceeded.

With another long exhale, Natalie put the SUV in Drive and started down the road.

Natalie hoped she was making the right choice. The last thing she wanted was to put anyone at the ranch in danger or to expose what they really did.

That's why she knew she needed to let Charlie handle this.

Even though Joshua was officially part of her crew, everything at the ranch fell under Charlie's leadership.

As Natalie headed down the road, she stole another glance at Joshua. His eyes looked glazed, and he still held his side.

He should have never left the hospital.

But after seeing those men come after him, it wasn't exactly as if Natalie could blame him for fleeing.

She cleared her throat. "Are you feeling okay?"

"Yeah, I'm fine."

But he didn't sound convincing.

A few moments later, when Natalie spotted a gas station, she pulled into it. She might as well fill up while she was here. Plus, Joshua could probably use some juice or a snack. Maybe even some Tylenol.

She cut the engine and turned to him. "Why don't you grab something inside while I top off the tank?"

He glanced at her a long moment before nodding and opening his door.

Once he was inside, she pumped the gas and then called Charlie to give her a quick update on what had happened.

Charlie listened to everything before agreeing that bringing Joshua back to the ranch to talk to her was the right choice. But Natalie knew by the sound of Charlie's voice that she wasn't exactly happy with this new turn of events.

After Natalie ended the call, her phone buzzed.

When she looked at her screen, her heart skipped a beat.

It was another video. From the same number that had sent her the other one.

She glanced around, saw that no one was watching, and then clicked on it.

Another dark, grainy video filled her screen.

This time, the images showed a group of people jostling in a small space. It was hard to tell exactly what was happening because of the camera angle. Everything was shaky, blurry, and too close.

But as the camera zoomed out, she spotted a moving truck parked near what appeared to be an old warehouse. Women whose hands were tied behind them were being ushered inside the back of the truck.

And one of the men doing so . . . appeared to be Joshua.

JOSHUA TOOK another sip of his orange juice as he stared out the window. He'd bought some Tylenol and had taken a couple of them, trying to ward off the pain from his injuries. He'd also grabbed a sandwich and some water for Natalie. He could only assume she hadn't had much to eat all day.

Now that his head had cleared some, he kept thinking about the scaffolding accident. He had checked the frame and platforms out himself before using it.

Had the man who'd come into the lodge last night somehow done something to sabotage the equipment? Had the potential arson just been a cover for another crime?

And if it wasn't the man last night who had damaged that scaffolding, then who?

A theory lingered in his mind.

What if one of Tomas Herrera's guys had secretly inserted himself into the construction team? Tomas had enough contacts that he'd be able to make that happen—or he'd be able to pay off someone already on the team to do damage.

But why would Tomas want to shut down an operation like the one at the lodge? Would doing so somehow hurt Joshua? There were better ways to get revenge on him than sabotaging his jobsite.

Tomas had been one of the leaders of the Gemini Cartel, but the man had purposefully kept his distance from the other members—just in case the cartel was ever taken down. Now that the group had been dismantled, Joshua suspected the man was working to covertly put the dangerous organization back together.

Even if he wasn't, the man was certainly trying to track down Joshua after his betrayal. He wanted to make Joshua pay for helping a victim escape and for walking away from them. No one did that to the cartel.

No one who lived to tell about it.

So many thoughts swirled in Joshua's head.

The sun was beginning to sink below the horizon, casting hues of purple and orange in all directions.

He'd always loved a good desert sunset.

If only he could truly enjoy it now. But he couldn't. Not with so much on his mind.

He glanced at Natalie. "So . . . if you don't mind me asking, how did you get into general contracting?"

Her cheek twitched as she stared at the road ahead. "After I was honorably discharged from the Navy, I was looking for something to do. My husband had a very successful contracting business, and I started to tag along with him. I found I had a knack for organizing and planning—it's what I did in the military."

"Interesting."

"Keith started teaching me the ropes, and I eventually got my license. When we found out Keith had terminal cancer, he wanted me to take over his company. I knew I didn't want to do all the major projects he was taking on. I wasn't ready—nor did I desire—to do that. Instead, I looked for smaller projects."

"Smaller like the lodge?"

A smile tugged at her lips. "This is actually my biggest project so far.

When Charlie approached me with the idea, I couldn't say no. I believed in what she was doing, and I thought it would be a nice challenge—even more so because the project was out in the middle of nowhere."

"I take it that some of your husband's crew still works for you?"

She nodded. "A lot of them left—and I knew they would. But I kept a handful, and then I've built up the rest of my crew on my own. Not everyone wanted to come out here. It's a big commitment."

"Yes, it is."

Natalie glanced at him. "How about you? How did you get into construction?"

He'd known his questions would be reciprocated. But he had to be careful how he answered.

"After I got out of the military, I began doing odd jobs. I like new challenges, new places, new people. Something about the desert called to me, and when I saw this job opening, I figured I'd give it a shot."

"You don't seem like the nomadic type." Natalie stole a glance at him. "You seem more like the type to have a plan and develop steps to reach your goals."

She could read him more easily than he'd hoped . . .

"I did work in a corporate field for a while, and I hated being behind a desk. I went on to be a white-water rafting guide, to work at a ski resort, and to be a tour guide out in southern Utah."

"Always up for the next adventure, huh?"

"Something like that."

Joshua's spine straightened when he saw the headlights growing closer in the mirror.

They were the same headlights that had been behind them for the past twenty minutes.

He was sure of it.

Making matters worse was the fact that he and Natalie had pulled away from Las Vegas and were heading back to the ranch. They were far away from the city now, and the roads were much narrower and more secluded out here.

He supposed that could work to their advantage. At least, there were fewer people to injure if things turned ugly.

He shifted in his seat before twisting the cap back onto his orange juice and setting it in the cupholder. Then he glanced behind him again and frowned, a bad feeling pinching his spine.

"What's wrong?" Natalie glanced at him as if sensing his unease.

"I think we're being followed."

She checked the rearview mirror. "Why would you think that?"

"Those headlights have been behind us for quite a while now."

"How can you be sure they're the same headlights? Don't they all look the same?" She glanced in the mirror again and frowned.

"The headlights on that car . . . one is just slightly dimmer on the left side. It's barely noticeable. But it's there."

Natalie glanced in the mirror again, and her shoulders visibly tightened.

"Do you think that those four guys have found us again?" Her voice trembled.

The answer raced through his mind. "I'm not sure how that would have happened. We lost them. Unless they somehow knew this vehicle was yours and put a tracking device on it, I don't see how they would have found us."

"Your phone?"

He shook his head. "It's untraceable."

Her eyebrows flickered up as if that surprised her.

"I suppose it could be *my* phone," Natalie suggested. "But that seems like a stretch."

"It is possible. But I doubt it." Joshua glanced over his shoulder again.

He wasn't sure what exactly was going to play out in the next few minutes, but his heart thrummed as he anticipated the worst.

———

Natalie's back muscles continued to tighten.

Had those guys found them again?

She'd wanted to believe Joshua was wrong. But he'd been correct. One headlight *was* slightly dimmer than the other.

Would there be another chase? If there was, Natalie wasn't sure she'd be as lucky this time. She knew the fact she'd dodged that train had been a near miracle. There were no guarantees they would escape again.

As Joshua had said, no one else was on the road, and those headlights had been following behind them at a consistent speed for the past twenty minutes.

Sure, she had been a Navy officer. But high-speed car chases weren't exactly one of the things she'd been taught to navigate.

"I might need to use your gun," Joshua announced.

Her eyebrows flew up. "My gun? What are you going to do? Shoot out the tires of the car behind us?"

He shrugged as if the idea weren't crazy. "If I have to. I won't make any moves until they do."

The bad feeling continued to gurgle in Natalie's gut. She didn't like this. Not at all.

Her phone buzzed, and she glanced at the screen.

It was a text from Charlie.

She quickly scanned the short message.

The next moment, Natalie jerked the wheel and pulled off to the side of the road.

"What are you doing?" Heightened emotion edged Joshua's voice. "Do you want them to kill us?"

She glanced at him before throwing the SUV into Park. "You're going to have to trust me."

CHAPTER
FOURTEEN

JOSHUA STARED AT NATALIE.

What in the world was going through this woman's head?

And how exactly was he supposed to trust her? He had no idea what she was doing—except maybe trying to get them killed.

Or what if she was working for Tomas this whole time? Maybe *she* was the one who'd sabotaged that scaffolding. In his line of work, he'd learned to trust no one. He hoped he didn't regret the trust he'd already given to Natalie.

Because he hated making mistakes.

The driver pursuing them pulled off the road behind them.

Joshua turned toward her, his heart racing. "I need your gun."

Natalie shook her head, her chin jutting out in stubborn determination. "I'm not giving it to you."

"What . . . ?" She wasn't making any sense.

She opened her door and started to step out.

Alarm rushed through him.

Joshua grabbed her arm as adrenaline kicked in. "What are you doing?"

Her gaze met with his. "Like I said. Trust me."

He held back some choice words as she stepped out.

He wasn't going to let her do this alone.

With a scowl, he opened his door and stood also, ignoring the pain in his side.

As he did, he saw two men step from the vehicle and approach them. Their headlights blurred their features.

Were these Tomas's men?

The next moment, Natalie reached out her arms and pulled one of them into a friendly hug.

Joshua's back stiffened. What exactly was going on here?

Were they all bad guys or all good guys?

He didn't know, but at least no one had started shooting.

Taking that as a good sign, Joshua took a step toward them, hoping his choice didn't get him killed.

———

Natalie had wanted to keep Joshua on edge.

He was keeping secrets from her, and she wasn't sure if she could trust him.

That was why she hadn't told him everything that was going on.

But as he approached, she turned to him and extended her arm. "Joshua, meet Hayes and Ruger. They're ranch hands at Vanishing Ranch."

As their faces came into view, Joshua's features seemed to soften with recognition.

"Good to see you guys here," Joshua said. "I didn't realize you were out this way."

Hayes shrugged. "We were just finishing up a couple meetings in Vegas when we heard what happened and decided you guys might need some backup."

"How did you even know where we were?" Joshua's thoughts still raced.

"Natalie told Charlie when she called from the gas station," Ruger explained.

Joshua sent a questioning look her way, but she shrugged. She didn't owe him any explanation. In fact, Joshua was the one who'd gotten them into this trouble—not her.

"Anyway, considering what happened, we

thought it was a good idea to find you since you guys were out here alone," Ruger continued. "We're just going to follow you back to the ranch to make sure you don't have any more trouble."

Natalie watched Joshua's expression carefully.

His doubts seemed to be replaced by a short burst of frustration, followed by acceptance. "That's probably a good idea."

"All right, well . . . it's been a long day, and driving out here in the mountains isn't always the most fun." Hayes nodded to his vehicle. "Let's get going."

They climbed back into their SUV, and Natalie started the engine.

As she did, she felt Joshua's gaze on her.

"You could've told me," he muttered.

"Just like you're telling me everything?" she retorted with a flick of her eyebrows.

He frowned and crossed his arms. "I guess that's fair. Is Charlie going to tell you to fire me when I get back?"

"I have no idea."

That was the truth. Part of her wanted Joshua gone. Wanted him to be far away from her.

But another part was intrigued. Natalie wanted to know more about this guy. More about how he'd ended up here. More about what his true motivations were.

Natalie believed he really was looking for a woman. Was Bella Rivers really his cousin? What else was he not telling her?

Instead of diving into any of those questions, she decided to simply remain cautious.

Given time, the truth would come out.

She would make sure of it.

PART OF JOSHUA wanted to be upset with Natalie.

Then again, he couldn't blame her for keeping him in the dark.

Maybe the fact that she'd just handled the situation so well had impressed him just a bit.

As did the woman herself.

From the moment he'd laid eyes on her, he'd been curious. What exactly had brought someone like Natalie to the ranch? Out of all the jobs she could've chosen, why come out here to this desolate jobsite in the middle of nowhere?

In the summer, the area was stifling hot.

There was little to no chance of having a social life, unless it was with the people you worked with. Joshua had met the rest of the construction crew, and they didn't exactly seem like the types she'd want to be buddy-buddy with.

What would Natalie do when this job was over, and the lodge was built? What were her goals for the future?

Would she remain in construction or choose another path?

All the questions ran through Joshua's head, but he knew he wasn't in a position to ask her.

For one, Natalie didn't trust him. Secondly, he officially worked for her. Thirdly, it didn't seem fair to ask her to share all those things about herself while Joshua kept so much of his own life close to his vest.

It wasn't that he didn't want to share. It was that he *couldn't* share.

By the time they got back to the ranch, it was seven p.m. To Joshua's surprise, they pulled through the gates into the ranch itself, Ruger and Hayes still behind them. He'd halfway expected their meeting to take place at the lodge.

His heart pounded a little faster. He wanted to see exactly what was beyond these gates.

Was this where Bella had been taken? Was this place a part of Tomas's operation?

Even more so right now, Joshua needed to figure out exactly what he would tell Charlie about why he'd taken this job. Natalie seemed to buy his cover story, probably because it was mostly shrouded in the truth.

But there was far more to him than he had shared.

If the wrong people found out who he really was, Joshua would be killed in an instant.

Then what would happen to Bella? Her mom and dad were counting on him to find her, and he didn't want to let them down. Mostly, he didn't want to let Bella down.

Natalie stopped the SUV in front of a large building at the center of the space, and he climbed out. The area was set up with a Western theme—from the style of the buildings, to the old stagecoach on the side of the property, to the cacti adorning various buildings. Horses grazed in a pasture in the distance, and several guest houses lined the other side of him.

Charlie met them outside, an icy look in her gaze as she observed him.

No doubt the woman didn't like to be tricked.

That would make this situation even more complicated.

"I hear you and I need to have a long talk." Charlie's voice held a cool aloofness.

Monroe stood behind her, his muscular chest tight, and his arms crossed as if he were her personal security guard.

Joshua had a feeling he wasn't someone to be messed with.

Remaining composed, Joshua said, "We do."

"Then let's go into my office." Charlie flicked her head toward the building behind her.

Before they could step that way, a man and woman exited the building. The woman gasped and paused in front of him, pulling the man to a stop beside her.

At once, Joshua recognized her.

He felt the blood drain from his face.

What was *she* doing here? Did this simply confirm to him that this place was really just a stop in some type of modern underground railroad for human trafficking?

"You . . ." she nearly whispered as her eyes widened.

"Do I know you?" Joshua swallowed hard as he asked the question.

She stepped closer, still studying him without apology. "You're the man who saved me when Diego's men held me captive."

———

Natalie sucked in a breath when she heard Emily's words.

What in the world was she talking about?

Natalie didn't know all the ins and outs of the ranch like the other people who worked here. But her nerves practically stood on end right now.

Charlie's hands went to her hips. "It sounds like we have a lot of talking to do."

Natalie glanced at Joshua and saw him staring at Emily, with her dark curly hair and wholesome features. As he did, Mateo, Emily's boyfriend, moved closer to her, his muscles bristled.

Was that a flash of recognition in Joshua's gaze?

He swallowed hard before taking a step back. "I think you have me mistaken for someone else."

Emily swung her head back and forth, the motion leaving no doubt that she was certain about her claim. "I don't. You're the reason I was able to escape. You're one of Arrow's guys—or Diego, as some people call him."

Joshua swallowed so hard that Natalie saw his throat tightening. "Who is Diego?"

Charlie shook her head as she stepped toward them. "All of you. Into the conference room. Now."

They all filed inside, no one daring to argue. Charlie and Monroe. Natalie and Joshua. Emily and Mateo.

Natalie was more curious than ever as to what was going on here right now. She prided herself at being astute. So how had she let Joshua's hidden identity slip by her?

Had she simply been blinded by his good looks and charming smile? Had the possibility of having him on her team clouded her judgment?

She wasn't sure.

Natalie hoped she'd find some answers soon and be able to put this whole thing behind her.

Because right now, this wasn't looking good for her future here.

CHAPTER
SIXTEEN

JOSHUA FELT sweat trickling down his spine.

Of *course*, he recognized Emily.

Everything she'd said was true.

But how would he explain this to everyone without blowing his cover?

He was a trained operative. He knew how to handle himself in tense situations. But this particular scenario felt tricky.

Charlie didn't bother to sit down. Neither did Monroe.

Instead, both of their gazes were on Joshua as he sat at the conference table.

"Before we get started, I'd like to advise you to be forthcoming with your answers," Charlie started before her gaze softened as she glanced at Emily.

"Emily, would you mind telling me one more time how you recognized this man?"

Emily nodded, not appearing afraid of Joshua. That should work in his favor, at least.

"When I was abducted, the only reason I was able to escape was because one of Arrow's men came to me one night," Emily started, her neck visibly tightening as if the bad memories were too much. "I was afraid he was going to hurt me. Instead, he took off my binds, unlocked the door, and told me how to get to safety."

"Then when we took down that operation, you said you didn't see the guy who saved you present among the other suspects, correct?" Charlie's gaze remained intense as she stood in front of the group.

"That's right. I would remember his face any day." Emily looked at Joshua, her eyes pleading with him. "It was you. Don't deny it."

Joshua's mind raced. He knew the Gemini Cartel had been brought down.

He hadn't realized that the people here at Vanishing Ranch had anything to do with it. Was that a part of the redacted information in those files at the office?

Things just kept getting more interesting by the minute.

So what was Emily doing here? Had she

somehow gotten herself back into the whole human trafficking thing? Had he released her only for her to fall into another trap?

He frowned. That didn't sound right. She didn't look distressed. In fact, she looked well cared for. Maybe his initial assumption about this place had been incorrect.

Still, nothing made sense.

"Joshua, could you please explain to us why you were working with the cartel?" Charlie's sharp gaze pierced him.

He could at least say what he'd told Natalie. That was safe enough to share as he collected the rest of his thoughts. "Two and a half months ago, my cousin disappeared, and since then I've been searching for her. I fear she's been abducted and sold into some type of human slavery."

Charlie sucked in a quick breath. "Did you report her missing to the police?"

"Of course. But they . . . they're understaffed and backed up with tons of cases. That's when I knew I had to take matters into my own hands."

"So you went in undercover with the cartel hoping to find her?" Monroe shook his head as if that thought was unbelievable.

Joshua kept his posture stiff. "I did what I had to

do. I was determined to find some answers, and that seemed like a good way to do so."

Everyone still stared at him skeptically.

Rightfully so. The action wasn't normal.

Of course, there was more to the story—Joshua just didn't want them to know those details. He may not have a choice but to tell them, however.

"So let's say that's true." Charlie shifted in front of him. "I know you were in the military. I did the background check on you myself. So you, with your military experience, decided to help your cousin by going undercover in one of the most dangerous cartels in the world." Her eyes narrowed skeptically. "I'm assuming you didn't find her, but you did manage to escape. You're still alive and walking despite the fact you betrayed a ruthless cartel leader. That doesn't explain how you ended up here."

Joshua swallowed hard as he felt everything squeezing tight. "I caught wind that maybe Bella was here at the ranch. I needed to find out for myself if she was."

"So you disguised yourself as a construction worker and came here?" Charlie continued to stare at him.

"I heard there was a job opening, so I saw the opportunity and took it. I do have some background in construction. I worked some jobs in high school and college, so I didn't lie about that. I wasn't trying to betray anyone here. I simply want answers."

Charlie stepped closer and pressed her palms into the table as she leaned toward him, her gaze practically slicing him. "Who are you really, Joshua Madden?"

———

Natalie listened with rapt attention to the conversation, and her thoughts raced as she tried to process everything.

Right now, Joshua simply stared at Charlie as the question hung in the air.

Who are you really?

Mateo and Emily quietly crept from the room, seeming to know that they were no longer needed.

But Natalie couldn't stop thinking about Joshua being undercover with a cartel. The fact that he'd saved Emily.

Whatever he'd been involved in was fascinating . . . and slightly unbelievable.

Joshua shifted in his seat. "I told you who I am."

"And I don't believe you." Charlie remained leaning toward him, clearly not backing down. "There's more to your story. You have skills that the everyday military member doesn't. You survived being around some of the most dangerous men in the US. You've put together bits and pieces of things that have led you here, to a place that isn't exactly on the map."

She paused, and silence stretched through the air.

Finally, she leaned toward him again. "Let me put it this way. I have the FBI on speed dial. If you're jerking us around, we'll find out."

Natalie waited with bated breath to hear what Joshua would say.

So far, he remained quiet, his expression not giving anything away.

That's when she knew she had to speak up. "I've gotten two videos you might want to see."

She pulled them up on her phone and showed everyone in the room.

Tense silence followed.

"That's not what you think . . ." Joshua started.

"Then explain." Charlie crossed her arms and stared at him.

Finally, he shifted in his seat and exhaled. "Okay, I'll tell you the truth. But this information cannot leave this room. Understood?" He glanced at Natalie, Monroe, and finally Charlie.

Charlie lifted her brows as if she didn't appreciate his tone, but she nodded anyway.

"I'm a special agent for ICE. Part of my job is infiltrating human trafficking rings to free the victims. I was assigned to help take down the Gemini Cartel, but I betrayed them. Shortly after that, Bella went missing."

Realization rolled over Charlie's features. "I wasn't expecting that."

"That's the truth." His jaw thrummed with tension. "I fear Bella's husband is somehow connected with the cartel—or they made a deal with him—and Bella disappeared because of me."

"I'm going to come back to that in a moment," Charlie said. "You took a risk while you were undercover by releasing Emily. Why?"

"I overheard Diego talking about transferring her. Her time was running out. So I helped her escape. But I've had my eye on this place for a while, wondering if you were part of a human trafficking ring also. There you have it. That's who I am and why I'm here."

As his words hung in the air, Natalie felt herself reeling.

ICE? Was Joshua telling the truth?

Charlie had ways of finding out.

Until then, Natalie would need some time to process these new developments.

CHARLIE'S EYES NARROWED, and she shook her head as she stared at Joshua, not bothering to conceal her doubt. "I find all of this hard to believe. Especially since, like I said earlier, I myself did the background check on you."

Joshua could explain that . . . "Because I work for a federal government agency, they were able to come up with a fake background for me and make it look real. I *was* in the military, and I *am* originally from South Carolina. They kept the basics truthful. They just obscured the fact I was working with ICE."

"I'm going to need to verify that." Charlie eyed Joshua closely as if looking for any signs of deception.

"Of course." He'd expected them to want proof when he'd made his admission. "Confirming my employment could be tricky because of the nature of what I do. But you can speak to my boss. I'd be happy to give you his contact information."

"That's okay. We like to do things our own way around here." Charlie nodded at Monroe, and he left the room. No doubt to check on Joshua's story.

Hopefully, they would verify it quickly, and then Joshua could finally get some answers.

As they waited, quiet filled the room. He was sure Charlie was letting this awkward silence happen on purpose because she clearly had a lot of questions she could ask right now.

Instead, she wanted him to sweat.

Maybe even start rattling off more information.

The woman may not be a trained operative, but she definitely had the instincts for these kinds of things.

Then again, for all Joshua knew maybe she *was* a trained operative.

Finally, fifteen minutes later—fifteen minutes that felt like hours—Monroe returned to the room.

Charlie looked up at him. "Well?"

Monroe stood beside her and crossed his beefy arms again as he scowled at Joshua. "He's legit."

"Are you sure?" Surprise tinged her voice.

Monroe offered a quick but certain nod. "Yes."

Charlie leaned closer to Joshua again, her gaze

locking on his. "You tried to come undercover into my organization? You need to understand that I'm the one who calls the shots here."

"Understood. But when it comes to finding my cousin, there's not much that I won't do." Joshua shifted in his seat. "Now, are you going to tell me what you're really doing with the women you bring here?"

Natalie watched the conversation, practically holding her breath as she waited to hear what Charlie would say.

Right now, Charlie and Joshua stared off at each other in a silent battle of wills.

Finally, Charlie stepped back, and her hands went to her hips again. "We're not participating in human trafficking here, if that's what you're wondering. We help women in bad situations."

Joshua's eyes narrowed with caution. "What do you mean?"

"Through a network we have, we learn about women—sometimes men—who are in desperate situations. Women who are in relationships with abusive men and unable to get away because of various concerns—financial, physical, emotional. We help to remove them from the situation and give them a new start."

"So you're like a women's shelter?" A knot formed on his brow.

"I'd like to think we're a little bit more than that. We give these women new lives, almost like witness protection, just unofficially. They receive new identities. New jobs. New homes."

Every time Natalie was reminded about what they did here, a rush of pride filled her. Charlie and the gang here were doing valuable work, and Natalie was honored to be a part of it, even if it was just in a small way.

The lodge she was building wasn't for vacationers or tourists. It was specifically for women who'd escaped or been rescued from human trafficking. Women who needed a place to regroup. Charlie already had plans of bringing in counselors, physicians, and career advisors/trainers who could help give these women a fresh start.

So often, after women were rescued from human trafficking, they had nowhere to go and no one to turn to. They'd been taken away from their families —oftentimes families who wanted nothing to do with them. Though they were given a new life, so many often returned to that very life because they had nowhere else to go.

Charlie was trying to change that.

Natalie had to admit she was fascinated with their mission and had even briefly toyed with the idea of seeing if she could stay on to work at the lodge, after the construction was done.

Though she was a general contractor by trade, maybe it was time for another life change. She'd needed something to ground her after Keith died so she'd kept working in construction. Or maybe she'd felt the need to carry on his legacy as a means of remaining close to him. She wasn't sure. Emotions were rarely that simple.

But how long could she be a nomad? Would she ever try to put down roots again? Develop a support system around her?

Joshua pulled out his phone and pressed a few buttons before showing Charlie the screen. "Have you seen her before?"

Natalie knew that Joshua was showing Charlie a picture of Bella.

Natalie hadn't been around the ranch enough to know if Bella had been here at some point.

Anxiety thrummed through her as she waited to hear what Charlie might say.

CHAPTER
EIGHTEEN

JOSHUA WAITED for Charlie's response.

What if she said yes? If Bella had passed through here, that would mean she was given a new life and a new identity.

At least, he could be grateful for the fact she was okay.

But if she hadn't been here . . . then where was she?

"I need you to understand that privacy is of the utmost importance here." Charlie finally lowered herself into a seat across from him. "It's only because we're extremely secretive about what goes on at the ranch that we're able to operate. The moment word leaks about what we really do, uncountable people could undermine our reputation as a safe space."

"I understand that." Joshua kept his voice earnest. "But I promise you can trust me."

Charlie stared at him another moment before nodding decisively. "Bella was supposed to come here."

His breath caught. "What do you mean *supposed to?*"

A small frown flickered at the corner of her lips. "We had her lined up to come here. We had an agent in place who helped her escape and put her on a bus. But when she got into Winslow, she changed her mind and said that she didn't want to do this anymore. I called her and tried to change her mind. I couldn't."

"What?" His voice rose.

Remorse filled Charlie's gaze. "The thing is, I can't force anyone to stay here. I don't want to force them from one life of abuse into another life where I dictate everything they say or do. That's not freedom either."

"I get that, but—"

"I explained the stakes to Bella," Charlie continued. "She still said she wasn't ready for this, that she missed her husband, Grundy, and that she wanted to go back home. I had no choice but to let her."

Why hadn't Bella come to him?

Or had she?

He hadn't been able to keep his contact with the outside world when he was undercover. But when he escaped the cartel, he'd followed up on all the messages, emails, and texts he'd missed.

There had been several missed calls from Bella.

Had she been reaching out for help?

Remorse—and guilt—pounded inside him.

He should have been there for her. She shouldn't have needed to rely on strangers to help. If he'd been involved, maybe she wouldn't have changed her mind.

Certainly, more could have been done to help her.

When he'd reached out, that's when he'd discovered Bella had disappeared two days after Joshua fled the cartel.

"But she didn't go back home." Joshua's voice pitched higher as he stared at Charlie. "You could've made her stay for just a couple of days until she came to her senses."

"That would have meant abducting her. As tempting as it was, I can't do that." Charlie frowned, her expression tense.

Joshua studied her gaze, searching for the truth. "You're telling me that Bella was never here and that you have no idea where she may have gone?"

"As I said, she told us she wanted to go home. We tried to follow up with her afterward, but she shut us out. That's the response that some women have sometimes, and there's nothing we can do about it. Our resources here are limited. We do everything we can to help people, but they have to want our help first."

Joshua rubbed his temples. That wasn't what he wanted to hear.

As soon as he'd learned this place was a shelter, he'd hoped Bella had been here to receive that help and to get a new life.

Why hadn't she accepted Charlie's help? Why say she wanted to go home and then disappear? Where was she now?

———

Natalie saw the distress on Joshua's face and had to resist the urge to reach out to him and squeeze his arm. To try to offer some kind of comfort.

It was clear he deeply cared about his cousin and wanted to help.

This news must be devastating to him.

"This doesn't explain why someone is sending Natalie these videos," Charlie said.

"No, you're right. It doesn't. Someone obviously knows I'm here and wants me to be discovered."

"No idea who?"

"Maybe a cartel member. It's the only thing I can think of."

"Gemini disbanded."

"A man named Tomas Herrera is trying to piece them back together. That was the backup plan all along."

Charlie tilted her head. "Does ICE know about this? The FBI?"

"They should. I told them what I know."

Charlie finally straightened and let out a weary breath. "Look, it's been a long day, and it's getting late. I think we should all turn in for the night and get some rest. We can meet again in the morning and talk more. But right now, I have other matters I need to attend to."

Natalie had to admit that she wondered if Charlie's statement had something to do with Amberly, Charlie's daughter, who'd unexpectedly shown up here at the ranch a couple of months ago. From what Natalie understood, the girl had been quite a handful. She wasn't sure of all the details about the situation, but she was curious.

Natalie stood first, her chair scraping against the tile floor. "That sounds good."

Joshua stared up at Charlie, an unreadable look in his gaze. Finally, he stood also. "I would love to talk more in the morning."

Charlie nodded, sounding slightly exhausted. "We can do that. I'm going to have Jesse drive the two of you back out to the lodge, and I'll have Hudson take a shift there tonight. If you have any problems, call us."

Natalie paused by Charlie. "Did you have a chance to look at the scaffolding?"

Charlie glanced at Monroe as her jaw tightened. "We did. Someone sabotaged it, just as we expected."

More unease filled her.

"We cleaned up the scene, and I had my guys put up cameras. If anyone comes back, we should be able to see them this time."

That calmed Natalie's nerves a little. But someone determined enough could make sure they weren't identifiable.

CHAPTER
NINETEEN

JOSHUA HAD TOO many thoughts rushing through his head to sleep.

After Jesse dropped him and Natalie back off at the lodge with a promise Hudson would be here in an hour, the two of them stood outside Natalie's camper, facing each other in the dark.

There was so much he wanted to say to Natalie. She'd been a lifesaver. A real trouper. And Joshua could understand how she might feel betrayed by his secrets.

He'd never meant for that to happen.

He'd never thought he would feel close to anyone while working this job.

The fact that she'd put her life on the line for him and gone out on a limb left him feeling like he owed her *something*.

"I'm sorry you had to find out this way," he started, resting his hands in the front pockets of his jeans. "But I couldn't tell you the truth upfront. Keeping my cover is part of my job."

She stared up at him, trepidation in her gaze. "I guess I can understand that. But I'm still not sure how I feel about all this."

"I'd be the same in your shoes. Thank you for everything you did to help me today. I have a feeling this all somehow ties back to me, and for that reason I'm sorry. I never wanted to bring trouble with me."

She tilted her head as she studied his expression. "You really think that the cartel is still operational?"

Joshua shrugged. "It's a good possibility. When I helped Emily escape from the Geminis, they weren't happy. I knew I had to get out of there. If any of them ever found me, there would be a price to pay. Maybe I shouldn't have stayed in this area for just that reason. But when I heard they were busted, I figured I'd be okay. I suppose there's a chance they still have connections in the area, and someone could have reported me."

Her gaze sharpened as if she didn't like that answer. "You mean like someone on the team?"

"Maybe. Tomas Herrera was best friends with Miguel. He was a low-key member of the gang—but powerful. He was put in that position just in case anything ever happened. These guys are smarter than people give them credit for, and they had a backup plan. Part of that plan was, if the gang was ever dismantled, they would retaliate against everyone who ever turned against them."

"And you think someone on the crew could be working for Tomas?"

He shrugged. "It's definitely a possibility. The cartel could have paid someone on the crew to feed them information about me or to sabotage the jobsite."

Natalie sighed and glanced back at the lodge. "I know Hudson's keeping watch tonight, but I'd like to go check the lodge out myself."

"Seems like a good idea. I'll join you."

Natalie didn't argue. They started walking toward the building.

As they did, Natalie asked, "Now that you know Bella isn't here, what does that mean for you? Will you leave?"

He shrugged. "I don't know yet. I don't feel I can walk away from this place right now—though I would have if Charlie asked me. Someone clearly knows I'm here and wants to send a message."

As they stepped into the lodge, a noise sounded in the distance.

A clunk . . . almost as if someone had accidentally knocked something over.

That's when Joshua knew someone else was in here with them.

Someone hiding in the shadows.

If one of the people he'd betrayed was here right now, then he needed to find out. There was no time to play games, not when lives were on the line.

———

Natalie gasped and stepped back.

Who was here?

The same person who'd tried to burn this place down last night? The person who sabotaged the scaffolding? Maybe it was the men who'd chased them from the hospital.

Charlie said she'd set up security cameras. Why hadn't they been alerted someone was there?

Unless it was someone they expected to be onsite.

Or maybe someone who knew how to bypass the cameras altogether.

However, she couldn't rule out the fact Joshua could be right. Someone on the crew could've been paid off.

Before Natalie could say anything, Joshua started

across the room. He was going to confront whoever was in here, she realized.

Her heart beat harder, faster. She wasn't sure that was the best idea. However, he *was* a trained federal law enforcement officer. He should know how to handle himself in these situations.

But for some reason that didn't make her feel better.

It made sense that he couldn't have a gun on him while undercover. It would make the other guys too suspicious.

Maybe Natalie should have given him hers.

She swallowed hard.

She couldn't just stand here.

This was *her* project. She was the boss. She couldn't let anyone mess with this place.

But everything that happened had left her shaken. Natalie hadn't expected to have to deal with this as a general contractor. It wasn't one of the things Keith had gone over with her.

She withdrew her gun from her purse and cocked it.

If someone was in here, she and Joshua needed to find them.

Just as the thought went through her head, footsteps sounded in the distance.

The person in here was escaping.

She picked up her pace as she followed Joshua toward the noise.

As Natalie left the lobby area and stepped into the kitchen, darkness surrounded her.

She fumbled with the light atop her Sig until it popped on.

As the beam cut across the room, she studied the area.

She didn't see anyone.

Joshua must've passed through the kitchen and headed elsewhere.

Her nerves pinched as she glanced around the space.

Had the intruder come in here?

Natalie couldn't get trigger-happy right now, especially since she didn't know where Joshua had gone.

With her back to the wall, she glanced around the room, keeping her eyes wide open. Boxes full of kitchen appliances were stored against the walls as well as other boxes full of screws, wires, and tubing.

Someone could be hiding anywhere. Construction sites were dangerous in the daylight, but at night . . . they were an accident waiting to happen.

She slowly crept around the space, looking for any signs of movement. Her lungs remained tight, and goosebumps popped across her skin.

She reached the pantry and shone her light inside. She didn't see anyone.

Then she began moving toward the dining area.

As she rounded the corner, she heard a sound and gasped.

Then the boxes in front of her toppled over, hitting her like an avalanche.

She fell to the floor, her gun discharging as she did.

TWENTY

JOSHUA HEARD the gunfire and rushed toward the sound.

When he reached the kitchen, he saw the pile of boxes on the floor.

Alarm rushed through him as he hurried toward them.

Was Natalie beneath them?

He threw boxes out of the way as quickly as he could.

Finally, Natalie's face appeared.

"Are you okay?" His words came out faster than he intended.

She winced as if uncomfortable but nodded. "I think I'm okay."

"Did you shoot him?"

"I don't think so. Now . . . enough talking . . . go find him."

"Are you sure?" He hated the idea of leaving her.

She grimaced as she pushed herself up. Several screws fell out of her hair and clinked on the floor.

But she had strength and sureness in her gaze when she nodded. "I'm sure. Go. I'll be okay."

With one more glance at Natalie, he took off.

Joshua rushed outside, hoping to find whoever had been inside the lodge. Hoping that he'd see a fleeing figure.

Instead, various crewmembers had stepped from their campers. No doubt they'd heard the gunfire and had come to check things out.

Where had this guy gone? He couldn't have just disappeared into thin air.

But he could be a crewmember now blending in with everyone else.

Joshua bit down at the thought.

This guy was hiding—possibly in plain sight.

As Joshua stared at the crewmembers, he had to assume one of them was behind this.

———

Natalie managed to pull herself to her feet, despite her wobbly head. Her arms shot out as she tried to find her balance. Thankfully, those had only been smaller nail and screw boxes that had fallen on her. Anything larger or heavier could have done some serious damage.

A few seconds later, she straightened, grabbed her gun, and sucked in several deep breaths.

Once she felt steady on her feet, she hurried outside.

As soon as she did, she spotted Joshua standing near the campers staring at the crewmembers gathered there. Joshua blended in—and it was better that way.

If crewmembers thought he was receiving some kind of special favor from Natalie, they wouldn't trust him. But if he seemed like he was one of them . . . maybe he could find out some answers.

Many of the crew had some kind of light with them. From the slight illumination, she could see that everyone looked confused.

They must have heard the gunshot and rushed outside.

Whoever had done this was staring at her now, wasn't he? It was one of these men. That was the only thing that made sense.

She joined Joshua. One look at him seemed to prove they shared the same thoughts.

"Which one of you was in the lodge just now?"

She planted her hands on her hips as she turned to her crew.

She stared at the faces around her, daring anyone to lie to her.

Enrico had expectation in his gaze, as if he'd anticipated personal conversation before being called out.

Buster looked hungover with his drooping eyes and disheveled hair.

Pierre—whose name sounded eloquent, even though he was a redneck through and through—was running his mouth to everyone around him.

Chester was quiet, waiting patiently for an update.

Could any one of those guys be behind this? She hated to think of any of them as being guilty—especially those guys. They'd been with Keith and had been loyal.

But loyalty could shift, and betrayal could be bought.

Everyone shrugged and shook their heads as if they had no idea what she was talking about.

"Someone was just inside the lodge, and he pushed over a bunch of boxes on me. I need to know who." She dug in her heels, determined to find answers. But as she stood there, she felt blood trickle from her temple.

She quickly wiped it with her sleeve. She must have gotten a cut there when those boxes fell on her.

Again, no one said anything.

She stepped out farther, her gun still tucked into her jeans. "Somebody knows something. Even if you weren't the one inside, certainly one of you knows that your roommate wasn't in the camper for the evening. Who wants to start talking first?"

The crew glanced at each other, but no one volunteered any information.

Finally, Enrico stepped forward. "I was dead asleep when the gunshot woke me up. Pierre was already sitting up in his bed in our camper. He heard the shot too."

Slowly, that same story—or a similar one—circled through the crew.

Someone wasn't telling the whole story.

Which meant everyone was still a suspect in her mind.

Natalie repressed the heavy sigh that wanted to escape.

How were they going to finish this lodge on time if she couldn't trust her crew?

TWENTY-ONE

JOSHUA WAS thankful when Jesse and Hudson had shown up five minutes later.

The men had heard the gunfire and had come to make sure everything was okay.

Joshua and Natalie had explained to them what had happened.

Then the four of them had gone into the lodge and checked the security footage using Jesse's phone. Unfortunately, it was so dark in the lodge that they weren't able to make out the man's features.

Video footage showed that the intruder had then disappeared into the shadows behind the campers, where he could've easily gone into any of them.

They weren't any closer to finding answers than they had been before.

When Jesse left and Hudson announced he'd

patrol the area, Joshua and Natalie turned to each other. They were still in the lodge with one of the construction lights on. But there were too many opportunities here for someone to overhear them.

Natalie nodded to her trailer that served as the construction office, and they headed there instead. She closed the door before going to the small table and sitting there. Joshua sat across from her.

Joshua studied Natalie's face. She looked exhausted. She needed rest. She needed less stress.

Since when had Joshua begun to care?

Or maybe he always had. He may have been in denial, but from the moment he and Natalie had met, he'd felt a rush of attraction. The more he got to know Natalie, the more he wanted to know her.

He hadn't come here looking for anything or anyone other than Bella.

His feelings for Natalie made him feel off-balance.

"Someone should keep an eye on you after your concussion." Natalie frowned as she looked up at him.

"I'll be okay." He brushed off her concern.

She let out a long breath. "I'd say you could stay in my camper, but then we'd be the talk of the whole crew. I can't let that happen either."

"No, you don't want that." He ran a hand through his hair.

She blew out another slow burst of air from her lungs, clearly deep in thought. "How about this? I have a couple of cots I grabbed for some extra crewmembers when they came out to help with the wiring a couple of weeks ago. We can set them up in the lodge, and we can both sleep there. I'll set my cot on the other side of the room just in case you need anything. I'll also feel better if I kept an eye on the place. So maybe this could be a win-win."

"Sounds like a win-win to me," Joshua agreed.

But he doubted he'd be getting any sleep tonight anyway, especially if Natalie was that close.

Joshua had been lying on the cot for two hours, but sleep hadn't found him, just like he'd thought.

Instead, he turned over and jammed his pillow beneath him again.

Across the room, he spotted Natalie lying on her cot.

Based on the sound of her breathing, she'd managed to go to sleep.

Good. She needed to rest.

But Joshua had too much on his mind to do so.

So . . . it turned out Vanishing Ranch was like a

halfway house. Now that he knew, everything made sense.

The work Charlie and the gang were doing was noble not criminal.

Emily's face flashed through his mind. He still couldn't believe the woman was here, that he'd seen her again.

He'd been with the cartel the day she'd been abducted. She'd been thrown into a room in the basement of a house about twenty miles from Vanishing Ranch.

He'd overheard the guys talking and knew she was the daughter of a prominent California pastor. He also knew the woman was about to be sold online to the highest bidder.

Though Joshua tried to save as many people as he could, it wasn't possible to save all the women who'd come through the house. But something about Emily had spurred him to action.

He would have been killed if he'd been caught letting her go. But he'd done it anyway.

And he was so glad he had.

How had she ended up here? Had she walked the entire way?

Shortly after betraying the cartel, he'd withdrawn from his undercover assignment and had returned to

ICE with enough evidence to shut the entire operation down and put Diego Sanchez behind bars.

That's when he'd discovered Bella was missing.

He'd taken a leave of absence to focus solely on finding her.

That had led him here. He'd always thought it was interesting that the ranch was so close to one of Diego's hideouts. Joshua had wondered if that was a coincidence or not.

Natalie shifted on her cot, drawing Joshua's attention again.

He'd gotten a whiff of her vanilla scent earlier.

And he'd wanted more.

But he'd broken Natalie's trust when he'd come here in disguise. Would she ever trust him?

Joshua couldn't say with any certainty that she would. At that thought, he frowned and punched his pillow beneath him again.

It probably didn't matter. She was a widow. Who was to say she was even ready for a relationship of any type? Who was to say that Joshua was ready?

He'd had a few short-term relationships over the years. But no one had ever caught his eye like Natalie did. There was just something about her that had him fascinated.

Maybe it was the fact that she was all feminine,

yet she could also lead a construction crew and throw back to watch football in her downtime as well.

Sometimes, connections like this just couldn't be explained. But from the first time he'd talked to her, he'd wanted to know more.

His thoughts continued to wander. How had Tomas's guys found him at the hospital in Vegas? Though he didn't recognize any of the men specifically, he was certain it was them. There was something about the way they dressed and walked that made that clear.

One thing was for sure. Tomas's guys were closing in. Joshua could feel it in his bones.

And he had to figure out exactly what to do about it.

TWENTY-TWO

NATALIE AWOKE the next morning before the sun rose. She'd hardly slept any last night—probably because she had too much on her mind. She had, however, felt a little safer knowing Joshua was nearby. She'd heard Hudson stop by a couple of times to check on them also.

She pushed herself up in her cot and blinked several times as she tried to get rid of her mental cobwebs. Finally, her gaze stopped on Joshua.

He lay on his cot across the room, unmoving and breathing softly. But she had trouble thinking he was asleep also.

She probably stared a little too long at his handsome figure. His classic profile. His blond hair.

He really was a sight to see. She'd be lying if she

said the man didn't intrigue her. He was the first man to draw her attention since Keith.

Last night, when she'd thought he might say he was leaving, a surprising sadness had filled her. A sadness that didn't make sense.

She hardly knew the man, and she wasn't looking for any type of romantic connection.

So where were these feelings coming from?

She suppressed a sigh.

Right now, she had other things to worry about.

Quietly, she stood and glanced around.

Everything appeared as it was supposed to. The unfinished walls remained intact. Tools and extension cords and ladders were still stored in the corner. The boxes on the other side of the room sat unmoved.

She quickly hurried to her camper, remaining hypervigilant as she did so—just in case. She couldn't afford to let her guard down after everything that had happened.

She spotted Hudson patrolling the perimeter and waved him over.

"Any trouble last night?" she asked.

He shook his head. "None."

"That's good to hear."

"Let's hope it continues."

She told him thanks and then went to her camper to change and freshen up.

Flashlight in hand, she started on the one-mile walk to Vanishing Ranch. The sun was still down and there was a certain stillness in the air that she loved. No one else was stirring except for the horses in the pasture in the distance.

She needed to meet with Charlie one-on-one.

When she walked into the mess hall, she spotted Charlie in the corner drinking a cup of coffee. Despite the early hour, she looked bright-eyed and put together, as she always did. It didn't matter what time of day, Charlie was 100 percent on her game.

Natalie could admire that.

No guests were in here yet—it was too early at only 6:30. The guys taking care of the horses probably wouldn't be in for another hour. That would allow them some privacy.

Charlie waved her over. "Thanks for coming out. Why don't you grab some coffee or maybe a bite to eat before we talk?"

Natalie poured some coffee and grabbed a muffin before settling across from Charlie. She needed a little caffeine to get her brain going right now.

Natalie took a sip before saying, "It's been quite an eventful couple of days around here."

Charlie twisted her head. "You're right about that. It sure has been. Then again, there's never really a dull moment around here."

Natalie gripped her coffee cup with her hand. "I guess we have a lot to figure out."

Charlie slowly nodded. "You could definitely say that. As you can imagine, I'm concerned about the construction site."

"Me too. I can't stop thinking about everything that's happened."

Charlie didn't bother to hide the way she studied Natalie. "What do you think about Joshua?"

The question caught Natalie by surprise. She shrugged as she tried to form her thoughts. "I was skeptical about him at first, but if you say his story checks out, then I suppose the nuances I've noticed make sense. He seems extremely capable, knowledgeable, and intelligent."

Charlie nodded slowly as she ran a finger around the rim of her mug. "I agree. I did a little checking into his background myself last night, and I didn't see anything suspicious. He does indeed still work for ICE, although he has taken some time off right now."

"And his cousin?"

"That story also checks out. Bella Rivers has been missing for ten weeks. When she changed her mind about coming here, she headed back home. We tried to follow up, but she ghosted us. I'm going to send a couple of guys to South Carolina to look into her background. I want to see what we can find out about her."

"I'm sure if she'd made it home Joshua would know by now."

Charlie nodded. "Which makes me even more concerned about her."

"So you're okay with Joshua staying?" Natalie's voice held a hope that surprised her. "I mean, if he wants to," she quickly corrected.

What if he didn't want to stay? After all, it was clear Bella wasn't here. Wouldn't he move on?

Why did that thought disappoint her?

Charlie wobbled her head back and forth. "I don't like the fact he came here under false pretenses. But, given his story, I suppose I can understand what he's doing, and that it makes sense."

"You think we can trust him?" Natalie spun the question in a slightly different way.

"I'm not totally convinced of that yet—it takes a long time to earn my trust. But I'd like to find out what Joshua knows about the Gemini Cartel. Even though they've officially disbanded, he could have some inside information on them. He seems to know something about how Tomas operates."

"That would make sense."

"So . . . back to the construction site." Charlie leaned back in her seat, an almost distant look in her eyes, as if she wasn't thrilled with what she was about to say. "We need to shut it down for now."

Natalie's breath caught. "What? But . . . I know you had a timeline for the lodge. Even just a little delay could put us behind, and . . ."

"Believe me. I feel the same way. I don't want any delays. This lodge and what I want to do there is important and vital for so many people. But I also can't have the crew getting hurt. Until we know what's going on, we need to pause our work there. The last thing we need is for OSHA to get involved."

"For how long?" Were Natalie and her crew going to be out of a job? It seemed like a possibility. How was she going to break the news to them?

"I want to do some digging and see what's going on. I'm hoping construction won't be shut down for very long, that we'll be able to find some answers quickly. But I can't give you anything definite."

"Anything about Lou?" Natalie asked.

"He's in Washington State. He's not behind this."

"And Albright?"

Charlie frowned. "We're still looking into him. I don't have any answers for you yet. It's a matter of wait and see."

Natalie realized there was nothing else she could say. Charlie's mind was made up. And what she said made sense.

Finally, Natalie nodded. "Okay then. I'm supposed to meet with the crew this morning. I'll let them know."

"Let them know we'll keep paying them for now. We're just going to have to take that week by week, though."

Natalie's chest loosened just slightly. Good. A paycheck would ensure most of her guys would stay. She didn't want to find all new workers—not if she didn't have to.

But Natalie needed to figure out the best way she could give this update to the crew.

Joshua watched as Natalie walked back toward the lodge from Vanishing Ranch.

He'd heard her leave this morning, but he'd pretended to be asleep. He'd heard Charlie say last night that they would talk again in the morning, so he could only assume that's why Natalie had gone over there.

Now he was anxious to hear if there were any updates.

He'd already gone back to his camper and cleaned himself up, pulled on some clean jeans, a thick thermal shirt, and a canvas coat. Most of the other guys were still sleeping or inside their campers, and they'd stay there until they emerged for breakfast at 8:30 and got to work a half an hour later.

Joshua met Natalie as she reached the cluster of campers.

"Good morning." His breath frosted in front of him.

"Morning."

"You're out early. Is everything okay?"

She paused and took a sip of her water as the early morning sunlight grazed her hair. "As well as it can be given the circumstances."

"Did something else happen?" His back stiffened.

She raked a hand through her hair before looking up at him with a frown. "Charlie wants to shut down the construction of the lodge until we know what's going on."

Joshua's jaw ached—he'd been clenching it, he realized. "I hate to say it, but that's probably a good idea."

"I agree. I just hate to get off schedule." Her gaze wandered to the lodge behind them. "We need this place up and running."

"We do."

"This is Legacy Lodge: The Loretta." A certain amount of pride filled her voice. "Charlie is hoping to secure enough financing to build more."

"I'm curious about why it's named The Loretta?"

"Loretta was Charlie's mom's name. After her dad died, her mom remarried. Apparently, this guy looked like a superstar on the surface. But he gaslighted her, put her down, and treated her poorly. He didn't actually physically harm her, but Charlie is certain that part of the reason her mom had a heart attack and died is because of him. Therefore, this is The Loretta."

"It all makes sense now."

A weary smile feathered across her lips. "I guess it does."

He sensed Natalie needed a shift from the heavy subject. "I guess you need to tell the guys?"

Natalie frowned before nodding. "I'm going to get Enrico and have him gather everyone in the lodge so I can tell them. The good news is they'll still get paid, and the crew has a place to stay until we figure all of this out. That'll give us time to look into who might be responsible for this, hopefully without anyone else getting hurt."

Joshua studied her a moment, trying to read her tight features and pensive gaze. "You agree with me then? You think one of the crew is behind this? Maybe even working for Tomas?"

"I don't know about them working for Tomas, but yes . . ." Tension stretched through her eyes until she finally nodded. "Someone close to this project has to be involved in some way."

She had a point. This may or may not have anything to do with Tomas and any revenge he might be seeking.

Joshua had a feeling the Geminis had a contact at the Vegas hospital, and when he'd been brought in this contact had alerted Tomas.

It was the only thing that made sense.

These guys had eyes everywhere.

Everywhere.

Joshua let out a breath. "I get that."

"I just can't figure out who or why."

He mentally reviewed the crewmembers—just as he'd been doing every day since trouble started here.

Enrico seemed the most responsible of the group.

Buster was obnoxious but seemed harmless.

Pierre was a redneck with a mouth on him.

Then there were sixteen other guys who stayed under the radar. It could be any of them. He'd been watching each of them, trying to shake out anyone with ulterior motives.

So far, nothing.

Joshua shifted. "How about if you let me get Enrico for you? I'll tell him that we need to have a meeting. That will give you a few extra minutes to gather your thoughts."

"That sounds great."

Joshua strode across the dusty ground to Enrico's camper. But the man emerged just as Joshua reached it.

"Good morning, Señor. You're up bright and early," Enrico noted.

"We need to wake everybody up for a meeting with Natalie. They should be getting up now, anyway."

"Of course."

"I'll help you," Joshua said.

They went camper by camper, waking the crew up. But when he reached the last camper, Jeff's camper, no one answered.

Sometimes the man went out for an early morning jog. But if Jeff had done that today, Joshua felt sure he would have seen the guy.

Joshua knocked again, but there was still no answer.

He twisted the door handle and pushed the door in. "Jeff?"

Silence greeted him.

Just to be certain that the man wasn't just a heavy sleeper, Joshua stepped into the camper.

He saw someone lying in the bed at the back of the place.

But something about the way his body was positioned put Joshua on edge . . .

With muscles tight, Joshua stepped closer. "Jeff?"

As he reached the man's bed, he saw the blood gushing from a slit in Jeff's throat.

CHAPTER
TWENTY-THREE

NATALIE WATCHED as Joshua emerged from Jeff's camper.

From the moment she saw his body language, she knew something was wrong.

Then she saw the blood on his hands, and her head began to spin.

He met her. "I tried to stop him from bleeding out . . . it was too late."

"Jeff's dead?" she muttered.

With a grim look on his face, he nodded. "I'm sorry. I checked for a pulse. There was none."

"What happened to him?"

"Someone sliced his throat open."

She swallowed the cry that wanted to escape.

She was the general contractor for this project. The boss.

For that reason, she had to hold herself together, even—especially—in the face of turmoil and tragedy.

She grabbed her phone and called Charlie. This was all above Natalie's pay grade.

Then she tried to remain calm as she waited for her boss to arrive. Word had quickly spread and Natalie encouraged her crew to remain calm and to stay inside the lodge. She insisted she didn't have any answers for them yet.

Charlie, Monroe, and Mateo arrived in less than five minutes. As they inspected Jeff's camper, she paced outside the lodge and waited. Joshua stood close by, needing to be available since he'd found the body.

Unlike her, he seemed stoic. He'd washed the blood off his hands, and now he stood with his arms crossed watching everything.

The rest of the crew were waiting for further instructions. They didn't need to know exactly what had happened, although Natalie knew they suspected something serious.

Joshua suddenly reached out, grabbed her arm, and stopped her frantic pacing.

She turned toward him, her heart rate rising to a crescendo.

"Are you okay?" Joshua asked softly as he peered

at her. "You're looking awfully pale. Do you need to sit down?"

She waved him off, trying to ignore how her heart raced at his touch. "I'll be fine."

"At least take a sip of water." Before she could start pacing again, he handed her an unopened water bottle.

She twisted the top off and took a long drink as the winter sun bore down on her.

Then she put the lid back on, gripped the bottle, and began pacing again.

Charlie, Monroe, and Mateo emerged only a moment later, grim looks on their faces.

They all met in the construction office. They found whatever seats were available as they gathered in a circle.

"We're going to have to call in the local sheriff." Charlie's jaw looked tight—as did the rest of her body. Even her voice sounded tense. "Clearly, this isn't something we can handle ourselves, as much as I might like to."

Natalie knew Charlie didn't want the ranch to get any unnecessary attention. She couldn't blame her. Attention could lead to questions, and questions could lead to an information leak about what they were really doing out at Vanishing Ranch. They tried hard to stay off anyone's radar.

Joshua shifted beside her. "Look, I feel like I brought this trouble here. I'm willing to leave if that's what you need me to do. Maybe I'll take the danger away with me."

At his proclamation, Natalie realized she didn't want Joshua to go. His presence here brought her a certain measure of comfort. Even before she knew he was an ICE agent, something about him seemed steady and reliable.

Natalie turned back to Charlie, anxious to hear what she had to say. Would she send Joshua away? Ask him to stay?

Natalie had no idea.

Charlie remained bristled and contemplative for several minutes. No one said anything as they waited.

Finally, she released a breath and turned to Joshua. "I'd like for you to stay. I feel like you have a lot to offer us and . . . maybe we can help you too. I sent two of my guys out to South Carolina to look for Bella, by the way. I hate to think that something happened to her when we were so close to helping. If there's anything we can do to make it right, that's what I want to do. Bella has to be willing to go along with us, of course."

"Of course." Joshua shifted, not hiding the gratitude in his gaze. "Thank you for doing that. I'll stay for as long as you need me to, and I'm willing to help however I can."

Relief filled Natalie.

Relief? Why did she feel relief?

She wasn't sure. But she couldn't deny the emotion.

Instead of dwelling on her feelings, she switched to a safer subject—relatively speaking. "Did the security cameras pick up on anything?"

Charlie shook her head. "No, it was too dark. We clearly need to get more lights out here too. I didn't think things would escalate as quickly as they have."

Natalie glanced through the open door of the lodge and saw her crew inside. They stood in clusters talking to each other, no doubt theorizing about what had happened.

Which one of her crew might have been behind this?

That's what they needed to figure out. She hated to think any of them were guilty, especially since she'd handpicked them herself.

But, at this point, they were the only ones who made sense.

————

"How long do you think it will take the sheriff to arrive?" Joshua asked as he stared at the crew in the lodge.

"At least twenty minutes." Monroe glanced at the time on his phone. "The county sheriff covers such a large territory out here that it's almost impossible to depend on them. That's why we try to handle most things ourselves. Same for medical help."

"I feel like we should talk to the crew and find out what they know before the sheriff gets here." Joshua glanced back at the men inside and lowered his voice. "One of those guys is most likely responsible for this. And why Jeff? Did any of them have a beef with him?"

"Those were my exact thoughts." Charlie stepped closer. "But we need to be careful. We don't want them to all go running because then we *definitely* won't find any answers. And . . . we have no way of keeping them here—not without physically holding them, which I don't want to do."

"I feel like I'm the most obvious one who could find answers." Joshua shrugged. "I mean, I *am* one of them. That is, assuming you're okay with me keeping my real ID under wraps?"

"Absolutely." Charlie remained silent a moment until she finally nodded. "Okay. You're right. You should talk to these guys and find out answers. So why don't you do that? Natalie, some of them might talk to you, especially Enrico. While you do that, I'd like to document this crime scene and look around Jeff's camper a little more to see if we can find any evidence of what happened."

Natalie nodded. "It's a plan."

Joshua nodded also. "Let's do this then."

As they stepped back toward the lodge, worry pounded through Joshua.

The fact was, Joshua didn't trust anyone in this group—except Natalie and maybe Charlie and Monroe. But what if Natalie was the next target?

The thought of something happening to her made a surge of apprehension rise inside him.

He couldn't let that happen. Even though Natalie was capable, Joshua knew he'd do whatever he needed to protect her . . . which was just one more reason he wanted to go question the crewmembers himself.

Though Joshua's main goal for coming here had been to find out information on Bella, he knew that somewhere over the past couple of days that had shifted. While he still wanted answers, he also needed to know what was going on here.

And he needed to know that Natalie would be safe.

He glanced at Natalie one more time.

The desert seemed to be full of danger . . . danger that had become part of the dry, dusty ground beneath him.

TWENTY-FOUR

BEFORE NATALIE HAD BEEN able to press anyone for answers, the sheriff had arrived and taken over the scene. Natalie had to pause from questioning her crew.

But her thoughts couldn't stop racing.

She saw another opportunity as the sheriff talked to Charlie and Monroe.

She headed toward Enrico, who lingered alone and leaned against the lodge watching everything. No one else was close enough to hear their conversation—which made this the perfect opportunity.

"You doing okay?" Natalie started as she paced up beside him.

He shrugged. "I just can't believe this."

"None of us can." She lowered her voice. "Who could've done this?"

He shook his head, a grim expression on his weathered face. "I have no idea."

She glanced at the guys in the distance as they huddled in small groups before leaning closer to Enrico. "Say . . . was Jeff having trouble with anyone on the crew? Anything I don't know about?"

"You think one of the crewmembers did this?" He stared at her with surprise in his gaze.

She shrugged, trying to look casual. "I don't know for sure. But it only makes sense, right? If someone else had pulled up here, we would've heard it."

She remembered the man who'd come on the motorized dirt bike and how she hadn't heard him. She didn't bring that up.

Enrico shook his head a little too quickly. "I can't believe that. You and I both picked the members of this crew. None of them would do this."

"That's what I want to believe also, but we can't confirm that. We need some answers."

"Keith would be livid if he were here right now."

She swallowed hard at the mention of her husband. "He would be."

Enrico turned toward her, something unspoken in his gaze.

"What is it?" Natalie asked.

"I've seen you talking to the new guy," he said. "I'm sure Keith would want you to move on, but be careful of him."

She stiffened. "What do you mean?"

He shrugged, almost self-consciously. "I don't know for sure. I can't pinpoint it. It just seems like the two of you were getting close. There's something about him I don't trust."

"I'll take that under consideration," Natalie said.

"I hope I didn't overstep." Enrico gazed at her a moment. "I just know how protective Keith was of you. He asked me before he died to look out for you."

"You've never told me that before."

"I didn't have to until now."

She held back a frown, knowing she couldn't argue with his words.

Enrico dropped the subject and stared off in the distance, letting out a long breath.

"What is it? Do you know something?" Natalie leaned closer, determined not to let him off the hook.

"It's probably nothing." He rubbed a hand over his mouth and chin.

Her breath caught with hope. "If you tell me maybe I can help you sort through it."

"I got up last night to smoke a cigarette, and I

thought I saw Pierre step out of his camper. He didn't see me, and I didn't say anything. I assumed he was going to take a smoke break himself."

"Did he go toward Jeff's camper?"

Enrico frowned before rubbing some dust from his work boot. "He headed in that general direction. But I didn't see him actually go to the camper. It's probably nothing," he began to backtrack. "I don't want to throw someone under the bus."

"I understand. I don't want to either. But the sheriff is going to question all of us." Natalie had to somehow get through to him, and this could be one of her only opportunities.

"I know. I don't have anything to hide. I'll tell him anything I know. I just don't want to believe one of my guys did this." Enrico's voice started to rise as panic claimed his tone.

"We need to keep our eyes wide open," Natalie told him. "If you remember anything or hear anything, please let me know. Ultimately, the buck stops with me, and I'm not sure how I'm going to be able to sleep tonight knowing something happened to one of our guys."

Enrico nodded even though the motion was stiff.

Just then, the sheriff headed toward them.

Natalie straightened and braced herself for his questions.

———

As officials took Jeff's body away, Joshua stood in the lodge and observed everyone on the crew as they milled around. He searched for any signs of guilt.

But as he watched the rest of the crew, he realized they all seemed clueless. The scuttlebutt around him indicated that no one knew anything and everyone loved Jeff. There were no conflicts.

But that was impossible.

Natalie cleared her throat as she called for everyone's attention.

The group gathered around her in the unfinished lobby.

"As you know, we've faced a horrible tragedy here at the worksite today." Natalie's voice betrayed her as it contained a tremor of nerves. "Now we begin the difficult task of picking up the pieces and figuring out what happened. The sheriff will contact Jeff's family and tell them the terrible news."

"Who would want to kill Jeff?" Buster scratched his head as he asked the question.

She rubbed her hands against her jeans. "We don't know. But the sheriff assures me he'll get to the bottom of it."

Joshua wasn't willing to sit around and wait for

the sheriff to do his job. He was going to investigate this himself. His fists tightened at the thought.

"What about the murder weapon?" a worker named Chester asked. "Did anyone find it?"

Natalie's expression remained tense but calm. "Not yet. Not to my knowledge, at least."

Joshua felt badly for Natalie as he listened. Not because he felt sorry for her. He admired her confidence, but he could sense her nerves. He knew this was a hard conversation.

She was still trying to establish herself, and an incident like this could be difficult to overcome. Plus, he sensed that maybe she felt she had to prove herself or not do anything to tarnish her husband's name.

As everyone continued to talk, a thought lingered in the back of his mind, one he didn't want to voice aloud.

One of the Gemini's signature moves was to slice the throat of their betrayers.

That fact made him even more distrusting of the people around him.

However, he couldn't show his hand right now. He needed to let these guys believe he was on their side.

"This jobsite is going to be temporarily shut down

until the authorities find some answers," Natalie continued.

Murmurs erupted.

"Before you panic, you'll be paid for the duration," Natalie quickly interjected. "It might be a week or two. We just don't know yet. The sheriff said we all have to stay close, that we can't leave the area. But as far as I'm concerned, if you need to go into town to get away from the jobsite for a while, then that's fine. I just want you back here at night, so we know where you are."

"Are we all in danger?" Pierre asked.

Joshua saw Natalie's face tighten. She either didn't know how to answer that question or the answer that jumped into her mind wasn't one she wanted to share.

"That's what we're trying to figure out." She kept her head held high. "We're going to hire some extra security in the meantime so we can make sure nothing else like this happens."

"So for now, we're free to go?" Buster almost sounded hopeful as he asked the question.

Natalie paused for only a moment before nodding. "Yes, for now you're free to go."

Joshua watched as everyone dispersed.

He had an idea he needed to run past Natalie.

But he had a feeling that Natalie was already on the same page with him, even though they hadn't spoken to each other.

TWENTY-FIVE

NATALIE AND CHARLIE listened as Joshua shared his idea—that they should tail any crewmembers who left so they could get a pulse on who might be guilty.

"I was thinking the exact same thing," Natalie told him.

"Me too," Charlie agreed. "We need to see if anyone on this crew is up to something, and following them is the best way to do that. If a member of the crew was involved in Jeff's murder, then this person could very well be headed somewhere right now to meet with a possible accomplice."

"I'd like to help," Joshua said.

Charlie nodded, seeming okay with his statement. "Of course."

"There's no way I'm staying out of this either,"

Natalie said. "Besides, we'll need all hands on deck to follow everyone. Who do you think we should follow?"

Joshua didn't have to think about it long. "Enrico seemed to point the finger at Pierre. I say we start with him. Is that okay with you, Charlie?"

Charlie nodded. "That sounds good to me. It will be a while until the sheriff and his team wrap things up here. But let's get ready for action once we're released. I'll stick around and make sure everyone is accounted for."

"It sounds like a plan."

As soon as the sheriff left a couple hours later, Pierre and Buster wasted no time getting out of there. They jumped into Pierre's old gold Nissan truck and took off.

It would be hard to disguise the fact that the men were being tailed out here in the wide-open spaces of the desert. But then again, several other people were also dispersing at the same time, so hopefully it would be less obvious.

"Let's go," Natalie muttered as she nodded toward her SUV.

She insisted on driving since Joshua clearly wasn't healed yet. He hadn't admitted he was still in pain, but she'd noticed how he reached for his side on occasion.

Her head still throbbed, and her shoulder hurt from the attack the other night.

Her body had definitely taken a beating this week.

She eased off the pedal as she realized she was getting too close. She couldn't stay right behind Buster and Pierre as they traveled out of this valley and toward the mountains.

There weren't that many towns out this way, but it appeared they were headed toward the Lake Havasu area south of the ranch. She didn't know much about the area, only that it was a popular tourist destination and that the lake was beautiful with its turquoise waters.

"Tell me something about yourself," Natalie started as she stared out the windshield. "I'd say tell me something I don't know, but that actually covers a lot."

That got a soft chuckle out of him. "I suppose it does. Let's see . . . I was in the military for several years. Army. When I got out, ICE recruited me, and I went to work with them."

"Have you ever been married?"

"Never. Been in a few relationships, but none of them ever lasted. It's hard when you work most of your cases undercover."

"Makes sense. Where are you from?"

"South Carolina."

"And what do you like to do in your free time?"

He shrugged. "I don't have free time."

She stole a glance at him. "Really?"

"Really. But if I did, I'd want to get a dog. Maybe take up hiking or ax throwing. I do dream sometimes about what it would be like to have a normal life."

"That sounds normal enough." Natalie offered a quick smile.

Joshua glanced at her. "Now can I ask you a few questions?"

"Of course." She braced herself for whatever might come up. There were some subjects she just didn't like to talk about.

"You said you were married before?"

She glanced at the tattoo on her ring finger. "I was. But Keith passed from cancer."

"I'm sorry." Joshua's voice softened. "What was Keith like?"

She let out a breath. She hadn't expected that question. "He was great. He was on the quieter side —at least socially. But when he was on the job, he was totally the boss. No one dared question him. But he was also fair, and he listened to concerns. He was good at what he did."

"Sounds like a good man."

She rubbed her ring finger. "He was. When I was

discharged from the military, I felt so lost. But he helped me find myself again. He wanted to know I'd be okay after he was gone."

"It looks like you've done well for yourself."

"I've thrown myself into my work."

"I know what that's like." He paused. "I'm sure Keith would be proud of you."

A slight smile wisped across her lips. "I hope so. I feel close with him whenever I'm on the job."

"How did you end up out here?" Joshua continued.

His questions didn't seem pushy, just curious and relational. Besides, it had been a long time since she'd talked about herself. She'd closed herself off in recent years.

She felt herself loosening up. "I was assigned to a support station in Tucson—most people don't believe there are any naval facilities in this area, but there are. The two of us met at church."

"You're not from Arizona?"

"Missouri, actually."

"And what's next for you after this?"

A frown tugged at her lips. "Actually, I'm not sure. I've been thinking about that a lot. But I've committed the next two years here, so I have some time to figure things out."

"I see."

They chatted until finally more and more houses and businesses began to pop up around them and the streets became more congested.

As Natalie suspected, Pierre and Buster pulled into a parking space in front of the town's local watering hole.

Eavesdropping on what they were doing in there would be trickier in the small space.

But they needed to figure out some way to keep an eye on whatever it was these two were doing.

***

Joshua watched as Pierre and Buster pulled up to The Loose Lasso.

The two men climbed out of Pierre's truck and then paused by the door to the bar. They talked a few minutes before Buster turned and continued down the street toward the market.

Pierre, on the other hand, strode inside the bar.

"Should we split up and each follow one of them?" Natalie asked.

Joshua hated the thought of Natalie being on her own. It was too risky. He couldn't take that chance.

"We need to stay together," Joshua said. "I think Pierre is our best bet so we should follow him."

Natalie stared at The Loose Lasso in front of

them. "We can't go into the bar. We'll be too obvious."

His jaw tightened. "You're right. We can't. We'll stay out here and keep an eye on him from here. It's the best we can do right now."

"Won't we still be too obvious if he comes out?"

Natalie may have done many things in the military, but she clearly wasn't very well-versed in stakeouts.

"We'll stay out of sight, and we'll come up with a cover story just in case he runs into us."

She nodded although she still looked unconvinced.

As soon as Buster was out of sight and Pierre was inside, they climbed from the SUV and stood outside the bar. They made sure to remain against the brick wall and away from the windows just in case Pierre glanced over.

"What do you see?" Natalie asked.

Joshua peered through the glass. "He's at the bar with a drink. But he's not talking to anybody. He's looking at his phone, however."

"Okay. I guess we just wait."

"That's right. We wait."

The minutes seemed to go by slowly.

Finally, Joshua straightened. "He's on the move, headed toward the back of the bar. Maybe to the bathroom. But he could be heading toward the back door also."

"What should we do?" Natalie whispered.

"Let's head to the back of the building. Just in case."

They circled around the storefront. Just as they reached the corner leading to the back alley, Joshua spotted Pierre step outside to meet a man waiting there.

The man handed Pierre a wad of cash.

Instantly, Joshua's suspicions rose.

TWENTY-SIX

NATALIE'S EYES widened as she watched the exchange.

"Do you think that guy is paying off Pierre for killing Jeff?" she whispered.

"It's hard to say. But it definitely looks unsavory, whatever is going on."

They continued to watch the exchange. The two men spoke to each other in low tones.

The only reason two people would meet behind a bar was because they wanted to do something unseen.

That made this whole situation even more suspicious.

"What do we do now?" Natalie whispered, her nerves pulled tight. "Do we follow them? Pretend like we didn't see anything?"

Joshua shook his head. "No, we confront this head-on."

Her heart pounded harder. Certainly, she hadn't heard him correctly.

But the next moment, Joshua took off toward the two men.

She had no idea what the game plan was right now, and she hated being in the dark. But she rushed behind Joshua, determined not to miss any of this conversation.

"Oh, hey!" Joshua's voice sounded friendly and surprised. "Didn't expect to see you back here, Pierre."

Pierre straightened, and his eyes narrowed as he spotted them. Quickly, he shoved the money into his pocket and glanced at the man with him as if trying to send a silent message.

"Joshua . . . Natalie . . . what are you two doing here?" Pierre demanded.

Joshua nodded to some bins a couple of stores over. "We need to grab some spare boxes for some groceries we're taking back to the ranch. The market down the street told us to go behind the store to get them. We just happened to be back there when we saw you over here."

Pierre's eyes remained narrow as if he didn't believe him. "Is that right?"

"Small world, huh?" Natalie added, trying to sound natural.

"You checking out this watering hole?" Joshua nodded toward it. "Is it any good?"

Pierre nodded, still appearing annoyed by the interruption. "I like it."

Joshua's eyes fell on the man Pierre was meeting with. The guy was short—probably only five foot four—with thick dark hair and a heavy build.

Joshua had never seen him before.

He extended his arm. "I don't think I've met you before. I'm Joshua."

The man hesitated before taking Joshua's hand. "Ed."

"So now you know what *we're* doing back here, but what are you doing back here?" Joshua raised his eyebrows, his voice still amiable.

The two guys exchanged a glance.

"Nothing important," Pierre finally said with a casual shrug.

"That sounds suspicious." Natalie let out a teasing laugh.

"Oh, no, ma'am." Pierre adamantly shook his head. "It's nothing like that."

"Nothing like what?" Joshua asked as if confused.

Pierre glanced around as if fearful someone might overhear this conversation. Then he whispered, "If you think I'm back here because of something having to do with Jeff, then you're wrong."

"Just because we saw that guy give you a wad of cash?" Joshua questioned.

"It's not like that." Pierre's words came out faster.

"Then what's going on?" Natalie stepped closer. "What's the secret?"

"It's not really that big of a deal," Ed said. "I just didn't want anyone to see us."

"See you doing what?" Joshua asked.

As Pierre and Ed glanced at each other, Natalie felt certain they weren't going to answer.

———

Joshua wanted to keep this easy and relaxed. He didn't want to have to get tough or demand answers.

That's why he tried to be nice.

For now.

But he wanted to know what was going on.

He stared at Pierre, refusing to blink until the man decided to fess up.

Finally, Pierre let out a long breath and raked his hands through his hair. "Look, if you really need to know, I sell baseball cards on the side."

"What?" Natalie asked.

Pierre let out another long breath. "It's just a

hobby, but it gives me some extra cash. I don't like to mail them because I lost one that way once. Whenever I come into town, I try to arrange meetings. Turns out Ed's been trying to get up with me for the past week because he was coming through this area. It just happened to work out that I could come into town and give him this card. It's a 1990 Topps #336 Ken Griffey Jr. Netted me four hundred dollars."

Not a bad payout, Joshua mused. "I never would've guessed. You don't really seem like the baseball card type of guy."

He shrugged. "I used to play in high school. And I collected these cards. Got them for Christmas and my birthday. Had a really nice collection. Six boxes of them, in fact. A few years ago when I needed some money, I discovered that I could sell some of the valuable ones I had."

"So you've been doing this for a while?" Natalie asked.

"That's right. I can send you my page on eBay if that would make you feel better. But I have quite the side business going on." He shrugged. "After my divorce I needed some more money so I could make my child support payments."

"You have a child?" Joshua asked.

"Ashley. She's ten. Being in construction isn't always a very consistent job. That's why I started selling these off. It gives me a little extra cash and ensures my little girl has enough money to buy some new clothes occasionally and get some ice cream when she's out."

Joshua believed his story. He sounded legit.

As if to confirm it, Ed pulled the card out of his pocket and showed it to him. "It might sound crazy, but sometimes meeting in public with valuables can be risky. I prefer to do these types of deals in private. That's the only reason we're back here." He paused and glanced at all of them. "What's the big deal anyway?"

They all exchanged glances, but no one said anything.

Finally, Joshua nodded back toward the grocery store. "We need to go get those boxes. I'm sorry that we interrupted you."

"Yeah, whatever, man." Pierre shrugged, obviously irritated.

Joshua put his hand on the small of Natalie's back and led her back toward the grocery store.

He figured Pierre hadn't bought their story.

But it didn't matter too much.

He didn't think Pierre was the killer.

Maybe they should've followed Buster after all.

TWENTY-SEVEN

NATALIE WAITED until they were out of earshot before she said anything to Joshua.

"Baseball cards, huh? Who would've thought?"

"I know. I sure didn't. But I think he was telling the truth."

"I do too. So what do we do now?"

Joshua paused and let out a deep, almost burdened breath. "Maybe some of the others are having better luck. And there's always Buster."

"We could go into the market and see if we can find him. See what he's doing."

"That's probably our best bet right now."

As they started walking toward the front door of the place, Joshua stopped. He pulled Natalie back behind the corner and against the brick wall.

"What are you doing?" Questions raced through Natalie's head.

"It's one of the Gemini guys." Joshua kept his voice low.

"What?" Her pitch climbed. "The Gemini Cartel? Inside the store?"

"No, on the street. Around the corner." He peered that way again. "Even though the cartel disbanded, their reach was wide. They obviously couldn't arrest everyone—it would have been hundreds of people. That guy right there used to work with them."

"You think he'd recognize you?"

"I know he would. We were together at that house that was not far from the ranch. I have no doubt there's a bounty on my head right now after what I did to them."

Tension crept up her spine. "What are we going to do?"

He pressed his lips into a tight line before saying, "For now, we need to stay out of sight."

"That would be easier if my car wasn't parked all the way down the street."

"Let's just wait and see what he does."

Natalie peered around the corner. Sure enough, a man stood on the opposite street corner talking on his cell phone. On occasion, he glanced around.

She didn't think this guy had followed them here.

If he had, he wasn't acting like it. But the last thing she and Joshua needed was to run into one of the Gemini guys while in town. That would just make this so much worse.

Finally, the man turned and walked in the opposite direction.

Natalie's shoulders slumped.

Joshua scowled as he glanced back at her. "We need to get back to your SUV. Now."

They hurried down the sidewalk toward where they'd parked in front of The Loose Lasso.

But just as they reached her SUV, a charcoal-colored truck pulled out onto the street and headed their way.

The window lowered, and a gun emerged.

Then bullets filled the air.

"Come on!" Joshua yelled.

He grabbed Natalie's hand and dashed away.

If they waited here, they'd be sitting ducks.

The guy must have seen him the moment Joshua came into sight. He must have called for backup.

Joshua pulled Natalie between buildings, knowing the truck couldn't fit between them.

But it would only buy them a little time.

He heard the truck squeal to a stop. Heard doors open. Then slam. Feet running.

This would not be a fair chase.

They darted from the alley. As they did, more gunfire filled the air.

The people around them screamed and ran for cover. Chaos ensued as cars braked and honked, and panic filled the air.

Joshua kept a firm hold on Natalie as he pulled her behind another building and then across the street to another set of shops.

He needed to put as much distance between these guys and them as he could.

Especially since they had military-grade rifles in hand.

More bullets flew through the air, and Natalie gasped beside him.

Joshua pulled her closer.

"We've got to move faster," he shouted.

She said nothing, only ran, following his lead.

He needed to figure out a place they could go where no other people would be around to possibly get hurt.

That's when he saw a good option.

But to get there, they would need to cross the street.

Dodging cars, he hurried across the busy intersection.

He looked back just in time to see one of the men stop on the other side and raise his gun.

"Get down!" He pushed on Natalie's shoulders.

Just as he did, more bullets flew.

Behind him, he heard the crunch of metal. Cars collided with each other.

He prayed that since nobody was going fast no one had been injured. That they were just fender benders.

The accidents might block the streets long enough for them to get away.

Joshua glanced at the spot he wanted to reach.

Still moving quickly, they finally reached it.

An old salvage shop.

He didn't bother to go inside. Outside was a plethora of old metal junk, including tractors, windmills, a couple of cars, and a deconstructed shed.

He pulled Natalie behind a large, rusty tractor.

Then they ducked.

Because they couldn't keep running like this.

Right now, they needed to figure out another plan.

TWENTY-EIGHT

AS NATALIE HID behind one of the large wheels of the tractor, she held her breath.

It was just a matter of time before these guys found them here.

But she knew they couldn't keep running—for starters because her leg hurt and was bleeding.

One of the bullets appeared to have skimmed her thigh. Thankfully, it didn't go any deeper.

But the wound still stung.

"You were shot." Joshua glanced at her leg with a worried frown.

Natalie cringed as he touched the area around her wound. "It's just a scrape. It hurts, but I think I'll be okay."

He leaned closer as he examined it. "I don't think

it hit anything major. But we'll still need to have you treated."

"If we live long enough to do so."

He looked up, his gaze latching onto hers. "Don't say that. Let's keep our hopes up."

Natalie shook her head, struggling to remain positive. "I don't see how we're going to get away. There are at least four of them, and they're all armed. I have my gun in my purse, but it won't be much use compared to those automatic rifles they have."

"Just hold tight." Joshua placed a hand on her back before he peered out again.

"What do you see?" she whispered.

His muscles tensed. "One of the guys just walked into the fenced-in area."

Natalie's heart pounded harder.

As soon as those men found them, all the guys had to do was pull the trigger and she and Joshua would be dead.

Sirens sounded in the distance.

Not surprising.

With a scene like the one that had just transpired, it had only been a matter of time before law enforcement would be closing in to find the gunmen terrorizing the town.

But would police get here in time?

She flinched as she heard something clink.

The guy had opened an old metal shed, she realized.

He was getting closer. Probably only twelve feet away.

She pressed her eyes shut and lifted a prayer that they would be invisible, that this man wouldn't find them.

The man paused. Natalie could see his feet on the other side of the tractor—practically close enough to touch.

She waited for whatever was about to happen.

———

Joshua gripped Natalie's gun.

He hoped he didn't have to use it. But he might.

The guy took another step on the other side of the tractor.

All it would take was a few seconds, and this thug would round this tractor and find them.

Joshua braced himself to act.

Then, as the sirens became louder, the man paused.

Muttered something beneath his breath.

The next second, he took off in a run in the opposite direction.

Joshua released the breath he'd been holding.

Law enforcement had spooked this guy.

Just in time.

A few seconds difference, and Joshua and Natalie might be dead right now.

Joshua waited until he was sure that the guy was far away. Waited until the sirens were upon them. Waited until he heard the crackle of police radios.

Then he tucked the gun away and grabbed Natalie's hand.

They emerged from their hiding space.

But they needed to get out of there before the police found them. Cops would ask too many questions. He and Natalie would have to explain too much.

He didn't want that to muddy the situation—not if he could help it.

Keeping their heads low, they walked at a fast clip back toward Natalie's SUV. He searched the buildings and streets around them as they did.

There was lots of confusion. Lots of police cars. Lots of people hovering in the entry to buildings, trying to find shelter.

No one seemed to recognize them.

That was good.

Natalie needed to have her wound examined, but it could wait a few more minutes.

First, they needed to get out of here.

CHAPTER
TWENTY-NINE

NATALIE KEPT SEARCHING everything around her as she and Joshua walked back to her SUV.

She feared the gunmen were still watching, but she had a feeling they were long gone. As soon as the cops had shown up, they'd fled.

In theory, she and Joshua should be safe.

At least, she hoped that was the case.

That encounter had been so close. Too close.

She could practically taste the danger in the air. Her body was still tense as she anticipated feeling another bullet cutting through her flesh.

Her leg was sore, and she'd need to clean her wound. But that could wait. Things could be much worse.

Finally, she and Joshua reached her SUV and slipped inside.

No police approached. The officers were too distracted trying to find the gunmen to notice them.

So far, so good.

She handed Joshua her keys so he could drive. Natalie was in no state to be behind the wheel, but Joshua seemed to have nerves of steel.

He returned the gun to Natalie before starting the SUV. After glancing around one more time, he pulled onto the road.

They started through the city, the police presence heavy as officers searched for the gunmen. She feared an officer might stop them.

But many cars were fleeing the area.

No barricades had been set up—not yet.

Thankfully, they managed to leave the area of town near The Loose Lasso.

She let out a breath and leaned back in her seat, grateful that at least that hurdle had been climbed. "I can't believe that just happened."

"It was a close call." Joshua's knuckles were white on the steering wheel as he glanced around.

"The first guy must have seen you." She spoke her thoughts aloud. "Do you think he was in town looking for you? Or could this be a coincidence?"

"I have no idea."

She shivered and drew her arms tight around her chest. "Right now, all I want is to get back to the lodge. We've caused enough of a scene today."

"Agreed."

In a few hours, darkness would fall. The day had been taken up with Jeff's murder, traveling to Lake Havasu, and the chase through town—a nightmare she never wanted to live through again.

They still hadn't eaten, but maybe they could grab something on the way back to the ranch.

Maybe.

First, they needed to get out of this town.

She noticed as they left that Joshua was taking a different route, one toward a historic bridge in the distance.

"Mixing things up?" she asked.

"I thought it could be a good idea."

Natalie stared at what looked like an ancient stone bridge stretching across the turquoise blue waters of the lake. "That bridge looks so out of place out here."

"Have you heard the story behind it?"

"No, I haven't." But she would welcome something to distract her from her thoughts.

"This wealthy man—I forget his name—bought several thousand acres out here in the area surrounding Lake Havasu. He wanted it to become a destination for tourists. Around that same time, the London Bridge went up for sale."

Her eyebrows rose. "The actual London Bridge? From England?"

"Yes, the one stretching across the Thames River. It was sinking. So this guy bought it for more than two million dollars or something. Over the next few years, the bridge was dismantled brick by brick and brought over to Lake Havasu, where it was rebuilt and where it currently still stands."

"Fascinating."

"Isn't it?" Joshua slowed the SUV as he started across the antique bridge. "You know, you were pretty tough back there."

Natalie felt herself glowing at his words. "You think?"

"I most definitely do. Then again, I already knew you were tough."

She cast a smile his way before glancing out over the lake—a true oasis out here in the desert. It was gorgeous.

If only she were here to enjoy it.

The next instant, something slammed into the back of them.

Natalie's head began to spin as her SUV careened toward the edge of the bridge.

Pedestrians on the walkway stretching across the structure screamed and dove out of the way.

Another car had just rammed into them from behind, she realized.

Suddenly, the old brick guardrail beside them didn't seem sufficient.

———

Joshua gripped the wheel tighter.

He tried to counteract the spinning and regain control. It was no use.

Nothing he tried made a difference.

Momentum was stronger than any correction he attempted.

He and Natalie might as well be spinning on a sheet of ice.

Joshua braced himself as they neared the edge of the bridge.

"Hold on!" he shouted.

The rear of the SUV collided with the guardrail.

Natalie sucked in a lungful of air and screamed as the rail crumbled.

The vehicle teetered on the edge.

Then the SUV tipped.

The next instant, he and Natalie were falling backward.

And falling.

And falling.

Until the SUV slammed into the lake beneath the bridge.

In a matter of seconds, water began covering the windows.

Bubbling up from the floorboards.

Filling the SUV's interior with frightening speed.

"Joshua . . ." Natalie sounded breathless as she cried his name.

He had to figure out how to get out of this situation—and quickly.

He tried to open his window, but it didn't budge. The car must have some kind of safety feature that cut the engine and battery.

He glanced around. "Do you have anything we can break this with?"

"No . . . I don't think so. Can't you open the door?"

"We're already in too deep." He demonstrated for her, showing her how the water pressure trapped them.

Natalie began searching her glove compartment for something they could use to break out. Then her purse. Then beneath the seat.

Her motions were frantic and her breath shallow with panic.

"Let me have your gun," Joshua murmured, knowing their time was running out.

She scrambled to find it.

Instead of shooting out the glass, Joshua took the barrel and propelled the handle into the driver's side glass.

It shattered.

He shoved the gun into his waistband and glanced at Natalie. "Is your seatbelt off?"

She quickly unbuckled. As she did, cold water covered her legs.

"We're going to have to swim out. Right now. The SUV is going to sink quickly. Understand?"

Natalie nodded.

But she appeared to be in shock as she stared at the shattered window and the water pouring in.

PANIC RACED through Natalie as the water swallowed the SUV.

What if she couldn't get out? If she couldn't make it to the surface? If shock and fear paralyzed her?

"You can do this." Joshua's gaze locked with hers. "Come on."

Before Natalie could question him, he grabbed her and pulled her across his lap, shoving her toward the opening.

Water gushed into the car. The cab would be completely submerged at any minute. The more volume that filled it, the heavier it would become and the more quickly it would sink.

"You go first." A new urgency filled his tone. "I'm right behind you."

She sucked in a deep breath before he pushed her out into the icy cold water.

Kicking her feet, she glanced back.

Joshua emerged just as the SUV started to plummet deeper.

He quickly caught up with her and nodded toward the surface.

Natalie's lungs burned as she thrust herself higher.

Exactly how far down were they?

They'd only been underwater a couple of minutes.

But however long it had been, it was too long.

She needed air. Now.

The only thing keeping her moving was the reassurance she'd seen in Joshua's eyes. He'd said she could do this. He believed in her abilities.

She could too.

Ignoring the panic she felt, she pushed toward the sunlight above her.

A moment later, her head broke through the water.

She gasped in deep gulps of air as she treaded water. She couldn't fill her lungs fast enough. They were greedy, wanting more and more.

She kept moving, trying to stop shock from claiming her body or mind.

But it might be too late.

Trembles already overtook her, and her head spun.

Another round of panic tried to take hold.

Joshua broke through the water beside her, liquid flinging from him as he threw his head back and sucked in air.

The sight of him caused her heart rate to slow some.

He turned toward her, his voice raspy as he continued to gulp in air. "You can do this, Natalie. We've got to make it to shore. Okay?"

He must sense her distress.

She wasn't so sure she *could* do this. Her body wasn't cooperating. Her arms and legs weren't doing what she wanted.

Her mouth dipped below the waterline, and more panic filled her.

She was going under again, wasn't she? Her tired arms and legs couldn't keep her afloat. The cold was winning. The shock was taking over.

Her eyes drifted closed as she slipped beneath the surface.

No . . .

Keith's image filled her mind.

It was replaced by Joshua's.

Then it went back to Keith.

The next moment, strong hands grabbed her and pulled her back up. "Natalie . . . stay with me. It's going to be okay."

Joshua leaned onto his back before taking her in his arms and holding her against his chest.

Then he began to swim toward the shore.

Through blurry eyes, Natalie could barely see the spectators gathered on the bridge—which was farther away than she'd assumed.

She was thankful that Joshua was with her. She didn't think her arms would get her to dry land on their own.

She'd been determined not to rely on anyone. So why was she relying on Joshua now? Why did she even *want* to rely on him after this?

She knew. Because having someone to carry your burdens with you . . . it was a gift. One she'd forgotten about. One she'd insisted she didn't need. That she was fine on her own.

And she was.

But she could be even better with the right man at her side.

A moment later, Joshua slowed. "Almost there."

Still keeping hold of her, he stood in waist-deep water.

He reached beneath her legs and shoulders and lifted her into his arms.

A chill washed over her as her soaking wet clothes clung to her body and weighed her down.

Joshua carried her to the rocky shore and laid her there. He leaned over her, checking her for injuries.

"We made it," he reassured her, keeping direct eye contact. "Do you hear me? We did it."

Natalie sucked in several more deep breaths, trying to calm herself.

The only thing keeping her grounded right now was looking up at Joshua as he stared down at her.

"You did great out there," he murmured.

She nodded. At least, she *thought* she nodded.

Thank goodness for Joshua.

She closed her eyes as exhaustion hit her full force.

She'd had enough for one day.

Natalie was going to let Joshua worry about what to do next.

———

As Joshua knelt on the shore examining Natalie, tension formed between his shoulders, pinching the nerves there.

The people who'd done this to them were brazen and wouldn't let anything stop them from getting what they wanted.

He glanced around for signs of anyone suspicious lingering nearby. These guys could be watching him and Natalie right now, just waiting for another opportunity to strike.

He saw some boats docked on the other side of the lake. A parking lot not far away. Some shops in the distance.

But most of the people he saw were on the bridge, peering over the side in horror. They seemed to be focused on the accident that had just occurred. Some had phones out, recording the incident.

Sirens sounded in the distance.

If Joshua had to calculate it, the current had probably carried them about a quarter mile away from the bridge.

His gaze stopped on a man wearing all black who walked from the bridge toward them.

It was one of the gunmen.

Joshua felt sure of it.

Urgency filled his blood, and he glanced at Natalie.

He considered running, but he didn't think Natalie was in any state to do so. Honestly, he probably wasn't either. His side still hurt from his earlier fall.

As several cops ran toward them, the man paused before darting away.

Joshua released his breath.

At least, he was gone.

For now.

But this guy—or someone like him—would be back. Joshua felt sure of it.

It was just a matter of when.

NATALIE PULLED the blanket up around her shoulders and stared out the window as Mateo drove them back to Vanishing Ranch.

Mateo was a former *federale* in Mexico, and he knew all about the inner workings of the cartel. Plus, considering the fact they were the ones who'd abducted his girlfriend, he was invested in this situation.

She and Joshua had already gone over all the details with him.

Now, Natalie just needed some quiet.

She still couldn't believe everything that had transpired in Lake Havasu. The whole thing seemed like a living nightmare.

Thankfully, she and Joshua had survived.

But how much longer could they evade these people?

Her thoughts wandered to the events that had played out after the cops had arrived.

The police had taken their statements, and EMTs had checked them out.

They were told they were lucky. A few more minutes in that water, and hypothermia would have set in.

The wound on Natalie's leg had been stitched and bandaged. She hadn't told them it was from a bullet skimming past her. That would open a whole other conversation she didn't want to get into right now.

They'd also been given some dry clothing to wear and cups of hot coffee to drink.

The cops seemed to believe them when they said they didn't know who'd hit them on the bridge. That was the truth—they really *didn't* know. Nor did the police seem to tie together the fact that Joshua and Natalie had been the intended targets of the gunmen who'd terrorized the town earlier.

The good news was that the police said no one had been hurt during the incident.

Mateo had arrived in Lake Havasu forty-five minutes after they'd called, and he'd remained in the background until they were cleared to go.

Once in the car, they'd filled him in on what had

happened. He'd listened, his jaw tightening with every new detail.

Beside her in the back seat, Joshua reached over and gripped her hand. He didn't let go.

She sent him a soft smile, grateful for his presence.

One thing was certain: all the danger they'd gone through had pulled them close—and bonded them quickly.

Natalie felt as if she'd known this man for months instead of barely more than a week.

But the more she got to know him, the more she wanted to know. The thought . . . well, it terrified her. She didn't want to go through more heartache, yet here she was finding herself attracted to a man with a dangerous job that could very well get him killed.

She frowned.

Joshua and Mateo chatted as they drove, but Natalie mostly tuned the conversation out. She needed some time to get her head together. To take a few deep breaths.

Plus, the pain medicine she'd taken was making her feel out of sorts. As soon as she could, she'd stop taking the pills. She'd rather experience discomfort but be in her right mind.

She leaned her head against the cool window as exhaustion overtook her.

But when she opened her eyes again sometime later, her head rested against Joshua's shoulder and his arm circled her back, drawing her close. She nuzzled into his warm body heat.

Until . . .

Reality hit her.

What was she doing? And in front of Mateo at that?

She sat up straight, feeling a flash of embarrassment. She was so thankful the darkness concealed her face. "I'm . . . sorry. Did I . . . ?"

"Don't apologize," Joshua murmured quietly. "You obviously needed to sleep."

She ran a hand through her hair, fighting mortification. "I can't believe I was able to sleep after everything that happened."

"Adrenaline rushes are usually followed by a crash."

"What he says is true," Mateo added from the front seat.

Natalie leaned back in the seat. She did still feel exhausted. Maybe everything was catching up with her.

A few minutes later, they arrived back at the lodge.

In the past, Natalie hadn't been able to say this place felt like home. But it did now.

She'd never been so happy to see her little camper.

———

After showering and putting on some of their own warm clothes, Joshua and Natalie had hitched a ride to Vanishing Ranch with Mateo, where they were situated back in the conference room. Chef had made turkey club sandwiches for them as well as some baked potato soup and sweet tea.

Charlie and Monroe talked with them as they ate.

Joshua updated them on everything that happened. As he did, Natalie added her thoughts. But she still seemed dazed from everything that had happened.

"Well, I'm glad you guys are okay." Charlie's expression appeared tight with tension. "That was a close one."

"Yes, it was." Joshua took a sip of his baked potato soup. He hadn't realized how hungry he was until the homey aroma hit him once he walked into the mess hall. "I'm still not sure how they found us there."

"We're going to need to figure that out." A frown flickered across Charlie's face.

Joshua ate another spoonful of the steaming soup.

"What about the other guys? I know they followed crewmembers if and when they left. Did anyone discover anything?"

"No, unfortunately, they didn't." Charlie glanced at Monroe. "But Chester left."

Natalie sat up straighter. "What?"

Chester? The man seemed too meek and quiet to be behind any of this. Then again, maybe those were the ones you needed to watch out for.

Charlie nodded. "We thought he was going into town—Sienna was following him—but instead he kept going. Went through Vegas to California."

"Where is he now?" Joshua asked.

"He stopped at a hotel outside LA for the night."

Natalie crept toward the edge of her seat. "Is Sienna going to question him?"

"This time, we're actually going to leave it to the police," Charlie said. "Running, of course, makes him look guilty."

"Will you let us know if you hear an update?" Natalie asked.

"Of course." Charlie shifted and grabbed a folder. "In the meantime, I thought you'd like to know that we also have an update on Bella."

His breath caught, and he suddenly forgot about his food.

Joshua braced himself for whatever Charlie was about to tell him.

He prayed for good news.

His gaze locked with Charlie's as he asked, "Did you find out where she is?"

"WHAT DO you mean no one has seen her?" The question left Joshua's lips before he could stop it.

"I'm sorry." Charlie frowned. "My guys asked around, but it's like she disappeared into thin air."

"Which would be impossible." He let out a burdened breath and shook his head. "Sorry for the outburst. I guess I was hopeful for good news."

"I can understand that. We can keep asking around." Charlie shifted. "Do you have any reason to think that Bella or her husband were connected with the Gemini Cartel?"

He let out another breath. "Her husband, Grundy, is a truck driver, and he used to frequent this area. I suspected he was using his truck to do some illegal things—things like trafficking women. I tracked him once and thought I saw him meeting with a cartel member. But I couldn't be sure. Why do you ask?"

"It's nothing concrete. Just a gut feeling. Like I said—we'll keep asking around." Charlie locked gazes with him. "I'm not giving up on this yet."

"I appreciate that."

Before they could talk anymore, the door burst open. A teenage girl stood there, her arms crossed and eyes shooting daggers at her mother.

"Have I told you yet that I hate being here? Because I do!"

"Amberly . . ." Charlie warned as she turned toward the girl.

Joshua glanced at Natalie, and they both stood. This was their cue to leave. Whatever was happening right now was obviously personal.

"Amberly . . . I don't appreciate that tone . . ." Charlie started, her tough veneer unwavering.

"I don't care what you appreciate!" The girl stomped her foot and crossed her arms, laser beams coming from her eyes.

Joshua cringed.

He might step in. Tell the girl to respect her mom. But not only was it not his place, he was sure Charlie could handle herself. If she couldn't, Monroe had her back.

But he could still hear them arguing as he walked away.

He prayed for resolution because Charlie certainly had a lot on her plate.

———

After the meeting ended, Mateo drove Natalie and Joshua back to the lodge and dropped them off.

It had been a long day.

At least, Natalie would be able to rest easier tonight knowing that Mateo would be guarding the site.

However, resting sounded nearly impossible after everything that had happened.

After Mateo said good night and went to pace the perimeter of the site, Joshua walked Natalie back to her camper. They paused outside her door.

Silence stretched around them as they gazed at each other.

"I'm really glad you're okay." Joshua stared at her, his eyes drawing her in.

"I'm glad you're okay too." Her throat tightened as she said the words. "There were times I wasn't sure either of us would survive."

The corner of his lip tugged up into a wry smile. "You and me both. Listen . . . Natalie, I know the timing of this is off . . ." His voice sounded deep and throaty, and for the first time since they'd met, he almost seemed uncertain.

"The timing of what?"

"What I'm about to say."

Her lungs froze with anticipation. "And what's that?"

He stepped closer—close enough that she could feel the heat coming from his body. That she could smell his minty aftershave. That she could see every line of his face.

"You're a remarkable woman," he started as he peered down at her, intimately close. "I've been so focused on my job in recent years that I've forgotten about everything else."

"What would that everything else be?" Her heart thrummed faster.

"My own future outside of work. Relationships. Love."

"Love?" Her eyebrows shot up.

A slight flush filled his cheeks, one she saw beneath her camper light.

He shifted as he shrugged. "I mean, it's too early to be in love—don't get me wrong. But . . . "

She raised her head, hopeful about where he might be going with this. "Yes?"

Her throat constricted as he leaned closer.

He licked his lips. "Maybe it would be better if I showed you."

Just as he cupped her cheek, a clanking noise sounded in the distance.

Joshua dropped his hand as they both turned toward the sound, anticipating the worst.

They looked over in time to see a shadow slip into the night.

CHAPTER
THIRTY-THREE

JOSHUA STARTED TOWARD THE FIGURE, calling over his shoulder, "Tell Mateo someone's out here."

If someone was sneaking out of his camper to wreak more havoc, Joshua wanted to know who.

"Hey!" Joshua yelled as he jogged toward the figure.

But the man ran.

There was no way Joshua was letting this guy get away.

Mateo appeared beside him.

"I'll go this way." Mateo nodded toward the left. "You take the other direction."

Joshua headed right of the campers, trying to cut this guy off. He rounded the camper on the end, bracing himself for any surprises.

There were none.

But he spotted a man lingering in the dark behind one of the modular homes.

Mateo appeared on the other end of the campers.

Good. Backup was close.

With a glance at each other, they both moved in.

Then, using all the strength he had left, Joshua darted across the ground and tackled the man.

"Hey, what are you . . . ?" the man complained as Joshua held him down.

Only then did his features come into view.

"Buster?" Joshua muttered with surprise.

"What are you doing, man? I was just coming out here to take a smoke."

"Then why are you being sneaky about it? Why did you run?" Joshua stood and brushed the dust off his jeans.

Buster shook his head, eyeing both Joshua and Mateo with suspicion. "I didn't know who you were. I thought you could be the killer and you were coming for *me* now. I guess you could say I'm a little on edge. We all are."

"You were just coming out to take a smoke?" Mateo repeated, his hands on his hips and a skeptical look on his face.

"Yeah." Buster reached into his front pocket and

pulled out a cigarette and lighter as if to prove his statement. "I didn't think it was that big of a deal."

"Well, next time just announce who you are," Joshua muttered, trying to keep the irritation out of his voice.

"And what if it's not you? What if it's a killer?" Buster stared at him, a touch of fear in his gaze. "What happened to Jeff . . . it ain't right, man."

Joshua didn't know what to say to that. Instead, he muttered for Buster to go ahead and have his smoke break.

Then he turned back to Mateo. "We're not the only ones on edge. I think everyone is."

"And rightfully so." Mateo scrubbed a hand over his face. "No one wants to end up like Jeff."

Jeff's image filled Joshua's mind, and he fought a frown.

He knew Natalie was waiting to hear what had happened, so he excused himself and made his way toward her.

She hurried from her trailer when she spotted him, concern in her gaze. "What happened? Who was that?"

Joshua explained the situation.

She frowned as he finished. "I was hoping for something more helpful."

"Me too." Joshua studied her a moment.

She looked so tired right now—as she should be after everything that happened. But he was worried about her. This was a lot for anyone to handle. She certainly didn't sign up for all this when she agreed to be general contractor here at the lodge.

"Why don't you go get some rest?" He nodded at her door.

She shoved her hair behind her ear. As she looked up at him, their gazes locked, reminding him that he'd almost kissed her.

Joshua felt something stir inside himself that he hadn't felt in a long time.

But that almost-kiss . . . it had been impulsive.

And a mistake.

He'd gotten caught up in the moment.

This stop here in Arizona was a temporary one on his journey. There was no way he could stay here at Vanishing Ranch. His job took him across the US and gave him little time to have his own life. The agency . . . well, they practically owned him.

That meant any type of romance that might be kindling would only be temporary.

He didn't do short-term flings.

And a temporary romance probably wasn't what Natalie needed anyway. She'd already been through such a major loss.

He should have remembered that earlier—remembered that before he'd cupped her face. Before he'd started to share how he felt.

Disappointment—more than disappointment, closer to devastation—pressed on his chest.

Joshua stepped back, his heart in his throat, and shoved his hands into his pockets. "Good night, Natalie."

Confusion flashed across her expression. He wished he could explain.

But not now.

Maybe tomorrow.

They'd been through too much today to dive into this.

"Good night," she murmured as her gaze searched his.

Joshua turned and walked away, an unsettled feeling weighing him down.

———

Natalie woke up the next morning with a sense of confusion and dread.

Confusion because she remembered her almost-kiss with Joshua last night.

What had happened to cause him to change his mind so suddenly? He'd almost made it look like he was afraid to touch her. Or even worse . . . like he regretted what he'd been about to say.

Maybe it was better that way.

Maybe Natalie wasn't truly ready for another relationship. Maybe Joshua had ultimately saved her from heartbreak.

So why did she feel so disappointed?

She sighed and rolled over in bed, her thoughts turned to the dread she also felt.

What would today hold?

The rest of the night had been relatively uneventful. At least, *she* hadn't heard anything.

But to believe the rest of the day would go the same seemed foolish.

There was no need to put it off any longer.

She quickly got dressed and then stepped outside. At once, she spotted Mateo near the lodge and walked toward him.

"Anything?" She crossed her arms to ward off the early morning chill.

He shrugged. "No problems."

That should make her feel better. But it didn't.

She was practically holding her breath as she waited for the next shoe to drop.

Just when she thought things were looking up . . . something came crashing down.

But she didn't have time to dwell on that now.

Chef delivered a continental-style breakfast spread for the crew, and Natalie helped set it up inside the lodge. Slowly, crewmembers wandered out to grab muffins, donuts, and coffee.

She scanned the place until she spotted Joshua. She flushed when she saw him and looked away.

She should keep her distance. Getting close had been a mistake.

She would remain professional toward him instead—what she should have been all along.

Pushing those thoughts aside, she clapped her hands and gathered everyone around her.

The crew formed a semicircle around Natalie and waited for her instructions and an update.

Before Natalie could start, Enrico stepped forward, looking surprisingly anxious. "Can we get back to work yet?"

Natalie held back a frown as she gripped her coffee and stood in front of her guys. "Not yet."

"Then when?" Buster tore off a piece of his donut and chomped on it as he waited for an answer. "It's not really going to be a week or two, is it? I mean, it would be one thing if we got paid for a couple of weeks of no work and could leave this place. But . . ."

That was a great question.

Natalie swallowed hard before saying, "We're still waiting to find out what happened to Jeff."

"Do you think one of us killed him?" Pierre scowled as he waited for her response.

This wasn't where Natalie wanted the conversation to go, but she understood the crew's concern. They wanted answers just like she did.

She braced herself before responding. "I think someone here knows something they're not saying. Something that could lead us to answers. I know there's a certain loyalty among the crew. But this project will be on pause until we know what happened. Safety is our first priority. That said, eventually the funds paying us will dry up. If anyone knows something, I encourage you to talk to either me or one of the staff members at Vanishing Ranch."

No one said anything. They all stood there in awkward—yet emotionally charged—silence.

"I saw you limping earlier. How'd you hurt your leg?" Buster asked. "And where's your SUV? I noticed you didn't have it parked by your place this morning."

"And why does the new guy seem to get special privileges?" someone else asked. "You two have been hanging around each other a lot."

Her throat tightened.

Of course, the guys had noticed. They weren't stupid. But she hadn't been prepared on how to answer.

"I was injured yesterday while I was in Lake Havasu. I was in a car accident."

"Was that your car that went off the bridge?" Buster asked.

She hesitated only a moment before saying, "It was."

Questions began flying, so many that she couldn't understand anything anyone was saying.

She placed her fingers between her lips and whistled. "Quiet! There's no need for so much speculation right now."

"But your head was bleeding the other day also," Enrico pointed out. "Why are you keeping us in the dark?"

She glanced at Joshua, who stood close as if ready to offer support as soon as she said the words.

She sucked in a deep breath. "The truth is that we've had some vandalism around here and other suspicious activities—such as the scaffolding incident. We're trying to get to the bottom of what happened."

"What about you and that guy?" Pierre nodded at Joshua.

"Joshua is my employee." Her voice sounded cold as she said the words. "I went with him to the hospital, and we drove back together. I also gave him a ride into Lake Havasu for some groceries. He was with me when my SUV went off the bridge."

"Are you sure he's not the one causing trouble?" another crewmember asked.

This was getting out of hand, and she had to bring the energy in this room back down.

"I'm sure," she said. "I vetted him myself. All I want is for everyone here to be safe, and to get this lodge built. I'm doing everything in my power to make sure both of those things happen. Understand?"

Silence stretched.

Finally, Enrico spoke. "What's next?"

Natalie tried to loosen her shoulders, but she couldn't seem to do so. "Right now, we hold tight. We're hoping that the sheriff will have answers soon."

"We have to hang around here today?" Pierre sounded annoyed.

"No," Natalie told him. "Like I said yesterday, you're free to go during the day. But I do want you back here tonight."

Murmuring circled around the room.

Natalie sensed the unrest among the crew.

And she didn't like the feeling rumbling in her gut.

The feeling that more trouble was coming soon . . . and maybe coming from within.

CHAPTER
THIRTY-FOUR

NATALIE WATCHED as Joshua took a sip of his coffee and wandered over toward her.

The crew had dispersed, and Mateo had gone back outside to wait for his replacement to show up. Charlie had decided this place would now have round-the-clock security and had already made arrangements for that to happen.

Natalie turned over a bucket and sat on it while she held coffee in one hand and a prickly pear muffin in the other.

"I know that was a tough conversation." Joshua paused beside her. "But you handled it well."

"Thanks." She set her coffee on the floor, tore a piece off the top of the muffin, and slowly chewed on it. "Nothing about this is easy."

"You're right." He glanced at the unfinished space

inside the lodge. "I hate to see progress slow down on this place."

"Me too. But it's too dangerous to keep going. We can't risk someone else being hurt."

"We need to figure out who is behind this." Joshua took another long sip of his coffee.

"I agree. But with no one talking and with us trying to remain low-key, it seems complicated."

"It *is* complicated."

"What should we do?" Natalie looked up at him. "Certainly, you've been in situations like this before."

"We have to keep our eyes wide open, look for any signs of deception or anyone doing anything suspicious. Eventually, this person is going to slip up."

In other words, it would require patience. Normally, that was something Natalie had by the bucketload. But in this situation, she prayed for a quick resolution.

As footsteps sounded behind them, they both turned.

Buster stood there, shifting awkwardly, and pulling his hands in and out of his pants pockets. "Can I talk to you, Natalie?"

Natalie tensed at the man's cautious, almost guilty tone.

"Of course." Natalie stood from the overturned bucket where she'd perched.

Buster glanced at Joshua as if expecting him to leave.

"Do you mind if he stays?" Natalie asked. "He's helping me to sort through some things. You can trust him."

Finally, Buster nodded—though he still looked doubtful. "Okay then."

Natalie stepped closer. "What's going on, Buster?"

Buster glanced around as if to make sure no one could overhear. Then he said, "Listen, I didn't want to say anything. But now I realize I need to."

"What do you know, Buster?" Natalie could hardly breathe as she waited for his answer.

He swung his head back and forth. "Jeff and Pierre were arguing over a woman they met in Lake Havasu. That's really why Pierre was selling those baseball cards—so he'll have money to wine and dine her. He's been going to town on the weekends to meet her. The problem is Jeff was also talking to her, and the two of them had some kind of spat about it. I'm not saying Pierre killed Jeff or anything. But I just thought you should know."

Natalie stored that information away, needing to process it a moment.

"Thank you for sharing." Natalie shifted as she tried to remain composed and not jump to any conclusions. "It's definitely something we should be aware of."

Buster glanced around again. "I shouldn't say this, but . . ."

Joshua bristled as if wondering what else might be on his mind. "But what?"

"I've seen Pierre head to the hills on more than one occasion. He says he's stretching his legs and getting some fresh air. But I followed him once. He has some kind of metal container he's hiding out there behind a rock underneath an old shrub."

"Metal container?"

"Yeah. It's shaped like a trunk. Looks like it could be military grade or something. I watched him put something inside it. I waited for him to leave to check it out, but it was locked so I couldn't get inside to see what was in it. But I thought that was suspicious."

"Sounds suspicious to me as well," Natalie muttered.

That was *not* what she'd been anticipating hearing.

Was the man stashing drugs away in there? Or something worse?

Joshua stepped closer to Buster, his hands on his hips. "Can you show us where this trunk is?"

Buster glanced around, almost appearing fearful. "Looks like most of the crew has taken off already. So if you want to, I can take you there now."

———

Natalie told Hudson—who'd shown up while they'd been talking to Buster—what was going on. Then the four of them headed toward the hills surrounding this desert plateau.

It took Buster several minutes to remember the exact location of Pierre's trunk.

Natalie wasn't sure what to think of the situation. Why would Pierre go through the trouble of bringing a trunk with him, hauling it out into the hills, and hiding it? Why not just keep it in his camper? It seemed like it would be far less vulnerable in a camper than out here.

It was also strange that Buster and Pierre had gone into town together yesterday. If Buster didn't trust Pierre, then why had he traveled into town with the man?

The questions swirled in Natalie's head.

"It should be right around the corner." Buster pointed to some boulders in the distance.

The four of them continued up the hill and over

some large rocks before they finally paused near a mature yucca plant.

Sure enough, a metal trunk—something similar to one a military member might use—was stashed there.

Hudson stepped closer to examine it. A small padlock secured the front.

He pulled his gun from his holster and then smashed the butt of it into the lock.

Natalie held her breath as he opened the box.

She leaned closer to peer inside, curiosity getting the best of her.

She held back a gasp at the sight of the bloody knife resting inside.

CHAPTER
THIRTY-FIVE

"WE'VE GOT to call the sheriff." Joshua stared at the knife and shook his head. "If this is the murder weapon—and it appears to be—then they need to know."

"Agreed." Hudson put the phone to his ear and made the call. A moment later, he slid his phone back into his pocket. "They happen to be working not far from here, so they should be here in about ten minutes."

"That's good news, at least." Natalie stood stiffly, clearly uncomfortable with this situation.

Hudson glanced around. "Does anyone know where Pierre is right now?"

"He said he was heading out." Buster shrugged as he offered the information.

Hudson's jaw tightened. "I'm sure the authorities will want to talk to him after they see this."

"I can only assume he went back to Lake Havasu. That seems to be the haunt he likes to visit the most. That's also where this woman is that Pierre is supposedly seeing, right?" Natalie looked to Buster for confirmation.

He nodded. "That's right."

Joshua ran a hand through his hair. "Let's say that Pierre is behind this. He had a spat with Jeff and killed him. You know what? Jeff was supposed to go up on that scaffolding the day I did. He very well could have been the intended target."

"But that still doesn't explain everything," Natalie reminded him without going into any detail.

"I agree."

"So are there two separate crimes going on here?" Natalie turned her back toward the sun as it began to beat down on her.

"It's a possibility." Hudson tugged on his cowboy hat to block the sun.

"If our theory is correct, and Pierre is guilty, then we have some answers," Joshua said. "But I still don't think we have the whole picture here."

Two vehicles appeared on the horizon, kicking up dust behind them as they headed toward the trio.

Hudson had dropped a pin on their location so the sheriff could find them.

Several minutes later, two sheriff's cruisers pulled up.

Hudson took the lead, showing the deputies the trunk and the knife, and explaining how they'd found it.

One deputy frowned as he lifted the bloody knife with a gloved hand. "I definitely want to talk to this Pierre guy. Where can I find him?"

———

From what Natalie understood, the county sheriff had called law enforcement in Lake Havasu to search for Pierre.

Police had located his truck, but he was nowhere to be found. Apparently, Pierre had gone into The Loose Lasso, but he'd left about an hour before the police arrived, and no one knew where he'd gone. Calls to his cell phone had gone unanswered.

Pierre must have suspected he was going to be discovered.

But running only made him look more guilty.

Thankfully, most of the other crew had remained gone for the day, so they hadn't seen all the sheriff's vehicles coming and going.

With Hudson keeping guard over the lodge—and Buster—Natalie and Joshua went to the ranch and grabbed some roast beef sandwiches so they could talk over everything with Charlie and Monroe in Charlie's office.

"We need to let the rest of the crew believe that Pierre has been the one behind these incidents," Joshua started as he picked up his sandwich. "Even if we all know there's more to it."

Charlie slowly nodded and propped her boots up on her desk as she leaned back in her chair. "I agree that's a good idea. We don't want them to know too much."

"There still is a possibility that we have a mole among us," Joshua said. "Someone connected to the Geminis."

"Yes, there is."

"What about Chester?" Natalie asked. "Any updates on him?"

"The police detained him and are bringing him back to the county so the sheriff here can speak with him. From what I've heard, he'd pleaded the fifth."

"I just can't see him doing this." Natalie shook her head.

"But we can't rule him out either."

Natalie didn't like where all of this was going.

The danger seemed to be multiplying.

"I also have an update on Albright," Charlie started.

"Who's Albright?" A knot formed between Joshua's eyes.

Charlie quickly glanced at Natalie, waiting for her to take the lead on this one.

"He's someone Keith worked with, but they had a falling out. I originally said he might be someone who'd want to ruin me . . . that was before I knew everything that I know now."

"Well, he happens to be in Kingman right now working on a project."

Her blood went cold. "Is he?"

"It's at the beginning phases, but I can't ignore the timing."

"He's a powerful man. I'm sure he has people who work for him."

"Even the cartel?" Charlie stared at her.

"I mean . . . maybe. He was doing some shady deals, deals Keith didn't want anything to do with."

"Did he tell you specifics?" Monroe asked.

Natalie shook her head. "He didn't. Keith tried to protect me from those things, I think."

Joshua shifted. "Any update on Bella?"

Charlie frowned and shook her head. "She seems to have disappeared off the grid completely. We still have some guys working on finding her. We talked to her husband in prison, but he didn't admit to knowing anything."

Joshua's jaw tightened. "Of course . . ."

The rest of their meal was mostly silent. Natalie let Joshua have his space to process what Charlie said. Finally, they finished eating and headed back to the lodge.

In a few hours, the crew would probably be arriving back.

Natalie knew they'd have questions.

Just as she, Charlie, and the gang had discussed, Natalie needed to stick with her cover story: Pierre was believed to be responsible because of a feud over a woman.

But deep inside, Natalie knew that this wasn't over.

AFTER ARRIVING BACK at the worksite, Joshua and Natalie spent some time in the lodge.

Joshua really wanted to get back to work on this place because he knew its value and he hated that they were wasting time.

He and Natalie didn't do much, but they both seemed to need to do something. To stay busy.

He'd noticed she was acting distant.

Was that because of their almost-kiss last night? He needed to explain himself to her.

But with everything going on, this just didn't seem like the time.

But her gaze wasn't simply as warm as it once had been.

They had cleaned and organized the inside of the

lodge, and Natalie had discussed with him their plan for moving forward at the site.

Natalie paused with a broom in hand and turned to him as they stood in the middle of the unfinished lobby. "What if Pierre is being set up?"

Joshua paused and turned to her as he chewed on the possibility. "You really think he could be?"

"I do. Buster could have been lying about seeing Pierre put something in the trunk. I just don't know. Everything seems so uncertain right now."

He stepped closer and squeezed her arm, although he knew his touch might not be welcome. "I know. I'm sorry you're in the middle of this. It's a lot. It pains me to think about how twisted some people's hearts are."

"The lengths they'll go through to get the things they want and to teach people lessons . . . it doesn't seem right," Natalie muttered.

"It's *not* right. But we live in a fallen world with fallen people. This isn't anything new to our generation. It goes all the way back to the beginning of time."

She nibbled on her bottom lip a moment before frowning. "You're right. It does. I just have a bad feeling in my gut."

"We'll figure this out. We just need to give it a little more time."

As he said the words, the construction lights went out around them.

They both froze.

"What . . . ?" Natalie muttered.

Just as Joshua flipped on the light on his phone, a shuffle sounded.

The next instant, someone stepped out, gun in hand.

———

"Enrico?" Natalie stared at her project manager. Stared at the gun in his hand. Stared at the hardness in his gaze.

No . . . he couldn't be involved in this. He was Keith's friend!

As Joshua started to reach for anything he could use as a weapon, Enrico raised his higher. "I wouldn't do that. Don't make me shoot."

Gone was the friendly man. In his place was a man who looked on the verge of a breakdown. Sweat dotted his forehead. His limbs shook. His stance appeared unsteady.

Enrico had been behind this the whole time?

The truth echoed inside her with a painful pang.

Followed by questions about their survival.

The power was cut. That meant the security

cameras were probably disabled also. Even though someone from Vanishing Ranch patrolled outside, Enrico walking into the lodge wouldn't raise any suspicions.

Besides, Ainsley—the operative from Vanishing Ranch who was on duty right now—was probably trying to figure out what happened to the power also.

She'd certainly figure out that something was wrong . . . but how long would that take?

"I didn't want to do this." The tremble in Enrico's voice belied his aggressiveness. "But the two of you were getting too close to the truth. I can't have that happen. Not if I want my brother to live."

"What are you talking about?" Natalie stared at him, trying to discern the truth.

"The Geminis. Four days ago, they kidnapped my younger brother. Said if I didn't do exactly what they said that he would die."

Her heart pounded even harder. "You've been the mole here? The one behind everything that's happened?"

Sweat trickled from his temple. "As soon as these guys learned that Joshua was here, they wanted answers about him."

"How did they even know I was here?" Joshua bristled and nudged himself in front of Natalie.

"One of them saw you in Kingman and began to shadow you. When he saw you headed this direction, he knew there was only one place out here you could go: Vanishing Ranch. When I went into town last weekend, this guy cornered me. Asked me about you. I told him it was none of his business. That night, I got a picture of my brother via text."

"Have you been telling them all the places we go?" Natalie tried to put the pieces together—and maybe buy some time. She had no idea what Enrico was planning for them right now.

"They told me to put a tracker in your purse. I slipped a coin into your purse—one with a tracker inside. I figured you wouldn't notice. Apparently, you haven't."

"No, I haven't." Natalie shifted. "But why me?"

"Originally, I was supposed to track Joshua, but I didn't have the chance. I figured you were the next best thing. I guess I was right."

"Are you the one who killed Jeff?" Natalie's voice quaked as she asked the question.

The gun trembled in his hand. "I had to." His voice broke. "I didn't want to. God knows I didn't. But I didn't have a choice . . ."

"Enrico . . ." Disappointment stained her voice.

"Jeff overheard me meeting with one of the men."

Sweat beaded on his forehead. "He thought he'd take advantage of the situation. He tried to blackmail me also. If he blabbed to everyone about what I was doing, my brother would die! I couldn't let that happen!"

Natalie sensed his desperation rising and knew she needed to calm him down before he did something drastic.

"Enrico . . . you don't have to do this." Natalie pleaded with him with her gaze.

"I do. I *do* have to do this if I want to get my brother back." The gun wavered in his hands. "I thought I put this way of life behind me, but trouble found me again. Crime has a way of grabbing hold and never letting go. Maybe it's in my blood."

"It's never too late to make things right." Joshua stepped closer. "You can work with us. We can bring these guys down and help your brother."

"I wish it was that easy." Enrico wiped the sweat from his forehead. His face twisted into a frown. "Believe me, it's not."

"Enrico . . ." Natalie stared at him.

"I'm sorry, Natalie. You were a good boss. Keith was a good friend to me. I never meant for any of this to happen . . ."

As soon as Enrico said those words, three armed

men stepped into the room, one from each of the surrounding doors.

One of the men dragged a woman inside with him, squeezing her arm tight and jerking her along next to him.

Joshua gasped as he stared at the figure. Then he muttered, "Bella . . ."

CHAPTER
THIRTY-SEVEN

JOSHUA COULDN'T BELIEVE his eyes.

Bella.

She was here.

In front of him.

And she was alive. Joshua wasn't sure what they'd done to her. But from a quick study, she appeared mostly unharmed. Her curly hair was frizzy and wild, dirt stretched across her cheek, and her shirt was torn. But overall, she seemed all right.

He wanted nothing more than to reach for her and fold her into his arms. He wanted to assure her that everything would be okay, just as he'd done when they were teens.

But with all the guns aimed at him, Joshua knew he couldn't do that.

The man holding her glared.

Joshua recognized the short, wiry man with dark hair. "Tomas . . ."

"You thought you were going to walk away from us?" The man clicked his tongue before mockingly shaking his head. "You should've known better."

Joshua's muscles bristled. "You didn't have to bring Bella into this."

He smirked. "Sure I did. I wanted to get revenge."

"Well, here I am. Now let her go and take me." Joshua raised his hands in surrender. "I'm the one you have a beef with. Not her."

At his words, Natalie let out a soft gasp beside him. "No . . ."

Joshua also wanted to assure her that everything would be okay. But he couldn't do that. Things might not be okay.

Tomas grunted and shook his head, indicating he didn't like Joshua's idea.

"How did you even get in here without us hearing you?" Natalie asked.

"You don't expect me to spill all my secrets, do you?" Tomas muttered with a nonchalant shrug. "We've refined our operations through the years. We have many talented people on our team. It's the only way we've been able to survive. We had a backup plan."

Bella struggled against Tomas's hold, sobbing as tears rolled down her face. "Joshua . . ."

His heart panged with grief and worry. He'd do anything to keep Bella safe—Natalie too.

Joshua took another step forward. "Take me."

"Oh, we plan on doing that."

"Then let Bella go," Joshua practically pleaded.

"I will. When I'm good and ready." Tomas nodded at Natalie. "But she's the one I really want now anyway."

Alarm spread through Joshua. "She has nothing to do with this."

"I disagree. I think she's going to be a valuable bargaining tool for us." He stepped closer to Natalie and ran his fingers through her hair.

Joshua bristled, every instinct inside him wanting to lunge at the man. "You're not taking her."

"Joshua . . ." Natalie's voice quivered as she said his name. "It's okay."

"Okay? It's not okay." Certainly, she wasn't considering going with them willingly.

He wouldn't let her do that. He wouldn't let her sacrifice herself to possibly save him. It wouldn't work that way.

This wasn't a movie. This was real life. And these men were dangerous.

They didn't care who they hurt as long as they got what they wanted.

"We can do this the easy way or the hard way." Tomas raised his gun. "But you need to decide soon. Otherwise, you're all going to die."

———

"We'll go with you!" Natalie said.

The bullet wound on her leg began throbbing.

And that had only been a graze.

How much worse would a bullet lodging in her chest hurt?

She didn't want to know. Didn't want to die.

She didn't want to see anyone she cared about die in front of her either.

That meant they were going to need to comply. There was no way out of this.

"Come on." Tomas nodded behind him. "We need to get moving."

Panic raced through Natalie. She knew she shouldn't go anywhere with these guys. But what other choice did she have? They were outnumbered.

She wasn't sure where Ainsley was. But a bad feeling lingered in Natalie's gut. What if something had happened to her?

Before she could dwell on that thought, one of the gunmen grabbed her arm and shoved her forward.

"Don't touch her," Joshua growled.

The man clearly didn't care as he shoved her harder. In fact, he almost seemed to find pleasure in manhandling her.

Another man took Joshua's arm and pushed him toward Natalie, toward the back exit.

Tension stretched through the air.

She prayed for some type of intervention. Prayed they could think of a way to get out of this.

As soon as they stepped into the darkness outside, a shout sounded.

Then another.

Then gunfire.

Backup was here. They'd been hiding out waiting for the right moment to help!

The man gripping Natalie's arm fired back. The deafening sound reverberated in her ears. Then he jerked her along with him and sprinted away.

More gunfire erupted.

"Move faster!" Tomas yelled.

Two Hummers swerved onto the scene.

The next instant, she and Joshua were shoved into one, and Bella into the other.

"Bella!" Joshua craned his neck back toward her.

But the other Hummer took off.

As Joshua bristled, one of Tomas's guards raised his gun toward them.

Heart pounding like a base drum in her ears, Natalie searched for Enrico.

She saw him by the door, looking bewildered. Confused.

"What do I do now?" he questioned one of the men, acting as if he expected to climb inside the vehicle. "What about my brother?"

One of the guards shoved him to the ground, leaving him behind.

Then the doors slammed.

They were trapped.

Cut off from any possible rescue attempts as they sped away.

WHAT JUST HAPPENED?

That was what Joshua kept asking himself.

Yet he knew exactly what happened.

He and Natalie had been abducted. Separated from Bella.

Enrico, no longer useful, had been left behind.

Had something happened to one of the guys from Vanishing Ranch? What had that shout been?

Joshua didn't know for sure.

He and Natalie were far from being out of danger. In fact, they had probably yet to experience the worst of all this.

These guys wanted Joshua to pay.

If Enrico had told them Joshua seemed to have feelings for Natalie . . . then they would use her to get to him. To make him suffer.

His heart lodged in his throat at the thought. That was the last thing he wanted.

The Hummer jostled as they sped across the desert, the driver not following any roads.

Joshua knew the guys from Vanishing Ranch would soon be on their trail. But first they had to get their vehicles.

His thoughts raced as he tried to think of a way to escape this situation. But in such a small space, it would be nearly impossible.

Besides, even if he did manage to subdue a couple of these guys, he knew there was no way to also protect Natalie in the meantime. And where were they taking Bella? Why the separate vehicles?

Were they taking Bella to a different location?

He would have to wait until they got to whatever place they were being taken to find out.

Then he'd have to figure out a way to get out of this.

If this were an ICE operation, he'd have guns. Backup.

But he was on his own right now.

At that thought, one of the men pulled out some black hoods. He shoved one over Natalie's head and handcuffed her as another man did the same to Joshua.

The hard, cold cuffs bit into his skin.

One of the men opened a window, muttering some choice words.

He began shooting. Probably at anyone who chased after them.

A moment passed.

Then more gunfire erupted.

This time it was from behind them.

The Vanishing Ranch operatives must have caught up to them.

Hope swelled inside him a moment.

Then he heard the guys discussing something. Barking orders at someone.

The next instant, an explosion sounded behind them.

An explosion?

Had Tomas's guys thrown a grenade?

His pulse quickened.

This wasn't good. Not good at all.

If they had used a grenade . . . what had happened to the guys from Vanishing Ranch?

Natalie wasn't sure how much time had passed before the Hummer came to a stop.

The gunfire had ended a while ago—but only after the explosion.

What had happened? What had Tomas's men done?

She didn't know, but she prayed the guys from Vanishing Ranch were safe.

She tried to pay attention to turns, but out here in the desert it was nearly impossible. The rough terrain threw off her equilibrium. She had no idea if they'd been taken north, south, east, or west. But she imagined they were somewhere secluded. Somewhere no one would find them.

Fear shivered through her. How were she and Joshua going to get out of this?

She had no idea.

She found some comfort in knowing that Joshua was a trained ICE agent. Certainly, he was capable. But some situations were impossible even for skilled professionals. She feared that this might be one of them.

The door opened, and cool air rushed inside.

The next moment, rough hands grabbed her. Pulled her outside so quickly she nearly tumbled onto the ground.

She heard Joshua grunt on the other side of her.

"Move," a deep voice said before shoving her forward.

The hood remained over her head so she couldn't see where she was going.

Her legs nearly gave out as they trembled with fear.

Natalie couldn't envision any scenario where they'd get out of this situation alive.

But she knew the guys from Vanishing Ranch would be coming for them soon.

Unless they had been hit by that explosion.

Maybe they hadn't gotten hit but had only pulled back a little.

That possibility brought her momentary comfort.

A door opened, squeaking on its hinges. Then she was pushed into a building of some sort. The musty smell inside reminded her of somewhere old and forgotten.

She heard Joshua being shoved around beside her.

Hands hit her shoulders and pushed her into a chair.

Her heart raced as she anticipated what might happen next.

A man jerked the hood from her head. She blinked, but there was no need to get used to any bright lights.

It was pitch dark in this space.

"Joshua?" her voice trembled.

"I'm here."

She turned her head toward his voice.

He was in a chair also. Not too far away.

She could only make out his shadow.

But somehow, just knowing he was close gave her hope.

Then she waited for whatever was going to happen next.

LIGHTS CAME on in the room, blinding Joshua as the bulbs were aimed at his face.

He squinted against the glare, searching for Natalie.

She was in a chair too, eyes closed against the intense light.

When his eyes adjusted, Joshua stared at Tomas and the semicircle of men surrounding them.

"What do you want?" Joshua asked.

"I need to make you pay." Tomas paced as he glared at them. "I need to make you an example for anyone else who dares to betray us."

"How are you going to do that?" Joshua asked through clenched teeth.

"I've been thinking long and hard about this. I

had one plan, but then I decided on another, better plan. It will take some work on your part, however."

"You were the one who sent those videos to me, weren't you?" Natalie's voice sounded dry and throaty with fear.

"As soon as Enrico gave me your name and number, I knew I needed to plant some suspicion in your mind. You didn't react the way I expected. But that's when I realized you must care about Joshua, which would make this situation ideal." He smirked as if enjoying this.

"Just let her go." Joshua fought against the cuffs on his wrists, even though he knew it was useless. "Natalie has nothing to do with this. Your beef is with me."

"Our beef is with *you*. That's exactly why we have her here." Tomas nodded at one of his guys.

"What are you going to do with her?"

The next instant, the man grabbed Natalie and pulled her from her seat.

The muscular man gripped Natalie's arms so tightly she let out a gasp. Panic welled inside her as he held her in place.

What was happening right now?

Undeniable danger thrummed through the air.

"What do you want from us?" Joshua asked. "What is this grand scheme that you have in your head?"

"I'm so glad you asked." Tomas smirked. "I'm going to need you two to become Mr. and Mrs. Ernest Hollis."

Ernest Hollis? The name didn't sound familiar.

"Why would we do that?" Joshua asked.

"Because I need you to go to the Grand National Bank of Vegas and retrieve something important from a safe deposit box there."

"Why us?" Natalie asked. "Why can't you do it yourself?"

"My face would be flagged. But yours won't. Who would suspect a sweet, loving couple?"

"You don't think people are going to get suspicious of us looking like this?" Joshua nodded at his dirty jeans and the bloodstain on his T-shirt.

"We have a plan for that also. This place isn't much, but we do have some water here. The two of you will get cleaned up. We have everything you need. Then we'll drive out to the bank. When it opens, you're going to do exactly as I say."

"And if we don't?" Joshua asked.

"Then Bella is going to die." Tomas held up his phone.

A livestream of Bella played. Tears rolled down her face as she stared at the camera with terror in her eyes, silently pleading for help.

Natalie's heart caught in her throat at the sight of it.

These men were ruthless, and this went deeper than she'd ever imagined.

JOSHUA'S HEART POUNDED HARDER.

How could this guy be so heartless? And why did they have to pull Bella and Natalie into it?

He knew why. Because the more pain they could cause, the better. The more lives they ruined, the happier they were.

Tomas began to pace again. "Now, in this particular bank, this is how it's going to work. You two will walk in and say you need to access your deposit box. While at an executive's desk, he'll need your IDs. We've already had those made for you. He'll ask you some questions—we'll review those answers on the drive there."

"Seems easy enough—as long as our faces match the photos." Joshua scowled.

"They will." Tomas paused. "But here's where it will get tricky. He'll need to check your fingerprints."

"What?" Joshua's voice rose with doubt. "That's a game changer."

Tomas smirked again. "Normally, it would be. But we have friends in high places."

What did that mean? Joshua didn't ask.

"He's developed a thin, glove-like product you can put on that will form to your skin and blend in. No one will know it's there. And the fingerprints should match."

"Clever . . . but if they don't?"

"Then we'll have a problem on our hands, won't we?" His gaze sharpened. "Failure is not an option."

Silence stretched through the room a moment.

"Is everything understood?" Tomas glanced back and forth between Joshua and Natalie.

Joshua's jaw tightened as he glared at the man. "It doesn't sound like we have much choice."

Tomas grinned with satisfaction. "I knew you would see it my way." He shoved his phone back into his pocket and then nodded at his men. "My men will take you to rooms where you can change and get cleaned up. But rest assured, you won't be left alone, so don't try anything."

"When do we leave?" Natalie stared at the man

with disdain. Sure, she was afraid. But she was still feisty also.

Good. That could work to their advantage.

Tomas glanced at his watch. "In three hours. Make sure you're ready."

One of the men jerked Joshua to his feet. Another man did the same with Natalie, but too roughly. She cringed with pain.

"Be easy on her." Joshua's voice sounded taut and edgy.

"I don't think you're in a position to tell us what to do." Tomas cast them a smirk. "Now take them to their rooms."

Joshua's heart pounded faster. He didn't want Natalie to be in a room alone with one of these guys. No telling what the thug would do to her.

What Tomas wanted most was whatever was in that safe deposit box.

That, and to kill Joshua.

But that didn't mean they wouldn't hurt Natalie.

The guy shoved Joshua into one of the rooms—an old bedroom, it appeared. Another guy dragged Natalie into the room beside his.

He prayed she'd be okay.

The man took Joshua's handcuffs off. Then he aimed a gun at him as he muttered, "Get ready."

Joshua would need to look respectable for this

outing. He saw a suit already laid out for him on an old mattress. A bucket of water sat on an old dresser with a washcloth hanging over the edge.

Not much of a bath, but it would have to do.

What was so important in that safe deposit box?

Whatever it was, it was worth going through all of this trouble.

Joshua paused by the suit and glanced around. Was there anything in here he could use as a weapon?

But there only appeared to be the stained mattress on the floor and the bucket of water on the dresser. Nothing else.

As Joshua pulled his shirt off, a cry sounded next door.

His muscles bristled.

Was that Natalie? Was that man hurting her?

In two seconds flat, his blood began to boil.

He couldn't let anything happen to her. Not if he had the power to stop it.

He glanced at the guard standing at the door.

The man was looking at something on his smart watch.

Joshua saw his opportunity and slammed into the man, throwing him against the wall.

He needed to get to Natalie.

Now.

———————

Natalie stared at the clothes that had been laid out on a rickety table for her—not only clothes, but shoes and jewelry too. And a wig.

There was also a bucket of water, a washcloth, and a hairbrush.

She glanced at the guard. "Some privacy would be nice."

"Can't do that," the brute muttered.

"What do you think I'm going to do? Run? There's nowhere I can go."

He grunted.

"Can I at least go into the bathroom?" She nodded toward the partially open door.

She dreaded to know what the room on the other side looked like. She could already smell a foul scent hanging in the air around it.

"Fine. But keep the door cracked.

She slipped inside, grateful for a moment alone.

The place was a dump, however. Rust stains on the sink and bathtub. A hole in the floor. Something brown streaked across the mirror.

Thankfully, the toilet lid was closed.

She didn't want to see what was inside.

Balancing on one leg, she peeled off her jeans.

The gunshot wound from earlier was still tender.

As the material from her jeans rubbed against her flesh, she let out a cry of pain.

Not even five seconds later, something crashed in the other room.

Her pulse heightened.

Was that Joshua? Was something wrong?

This whole scheme Tomas planned seemed crazy. How were she and Joshua supposed to get away with impersonating someone else and getting into that bank? If they were caught, they'd be arrested.

Maybe because of the circumstances, law enforcement would understand the position that they were in.

That they didn't have a choice.

But whatever was in the safe deposit box must be important. Important enough to kill for.

That fact also made her nervous.

She remained bristled as she heard more fighting in the other room.

She prayed that Joshua was okay. She wanted more than anything to check on him. To see how he was.

But she forced herself to remain calm. Joshua could take care of himself.

Not only that, but she wouldn't be much help against these men. They were bigger than her and trained for combat. They had guns.

She peeked through the doorway at the man standing guard. He held an assault-style rifle and stared at her. There was no way she would be getting past this guy. A sick feeling gurgled in her stomach.

"I wouldn't worry about him," the man muttered. "I'd worry about you."

Another wave of fear swept over her.

Finally, the noises in the other room stopped.

What if that was because they'd done something horrible to Joshua?

What if they killed him?

No, she realized. They need him alive right now and relatively unharmed. He *should* be okay.

As she continued getting cleaned up, tears pressed at her eyes.

She hadn't realized just how much she'd come to care about him.

But she did.

Even though the two of them hadn't known each other that long, thinking about her future without Joshua made life seem a lot dimmer.

She even thought that Keith might approve of him, and Keith was a man who was hard to please. But he'd always only wanted the best for her.

"You doing okay in there?" the guard called.

Silence still stretched in the other room, and more

tears flooded across her cheeks. Natalie quickly wiped them away. "I'm just peachy."

The man grunted.

Natalie picked up her pace.

The only way she would find out if Joshua was okay was to get out of this room.

Until then, she just had to pretend to be compliant.

FORTY-ONE

JOSHUA RUBBED HIS HEAD.

The man at the door had slammed his gun across Joshua's skull.

The blow had sent Joshua toppling to the floor and rendered him unable to fight anymore.

The only thing that comforted him was knowing no more sounds came from Natalie's room.

But the scenarios that had gone through his head . . .

He'd seen the worst side of people. There were images in his mind he would never get out. It was a hazard of the job—a hazard of working with human trafficking.

He'd thought there couldn't be a future between him and Natalie. That any distractions from his job could lead to more people being harmed.

While, in part, that was true, that same dedication put the people he loved in danger.

There had to be a balance.

He wanted to know what his future with Natalie would look like. Wanted to know if they could make it work.

He'd never felt more certain about that than he did now.

What if a career change was in his future? If there was a way he and Natalie could work something out?

Wasn't that what people did when something was important to them? They decided their priorities and then adjusted their lives to it. How much more so should it be that way when it involved another person?

Maybe, for once in his life, work shouldn't be the most important thing to him. Maybe he should focus on his own future.

Because he couldn't do this job forever. When his assignments were over, and all was said and done, he was going to be alone.

He wasn't sure where these thoughts were coming from. But they bombarded him now. With every aching pulse of his head, he couldn't stop thinking about Natalie.

"Stop wasting time. Get ready!" the man barked from the door.

Grunting, Joshua pulled himself to his feet, his head aching.

He couldn't attack the guy again. He wasn't even sure what he'd been thinking. He was usually so much more measured than that.

He had to keep a cool head if he was going to get out of this situation. If he was going to help Natalie get free as well.

For that reason, he went to the bucket of water that had been left on the dresser for him and began to wash his face.

He had to get ready for this misadventure he was about to embark on.

———

When Natalie left her room and saw Joshua sitting in an old wooden chair, her chest filled with relief.

He was okay!

Whatever had happened in there, he'd survived it.

And he *did* look better. He'd cleaned himself up. Put on a suit. Added some glasses.

Though he looked good in that suit, Natalie would take him in jeans or Carhart pants any day of the week. There was something about a blue-collar worker that got her every time . . .

Their gazes met, and Natalie saw the questions there.

Joshua was worried about her also.

And for good reason.

This situation was precarious.

His gaze flickered over her a moment. She self-consciously adjusted the wig of long, dark-brown hair she'd been given. Smoothed a hand down the black jumpsuit she wore with heels and jewelry.

She'd caught a glimpse of herself in the mirror before stepping out here, and she did look as if she'd been transformed into someone else.

Joshua gave her a small, reassuring smile.

The barely there gesture gave her the confidence to step forward and proceed with this whole scheme.

At least, they would be side by side through this.

"Have a seat, Natalie." Tomas paced in front of them, looking as smug as ever. "You two clean up rather well."

She sat in the chair next to Joshua, ignoring the man's comment.

"When are we leaving?" Joshua barked.

"Soon enough. I just need to brief you on several things."

He then explained their new identities, handing them new driver's licenses. A man she hadn't seen before came into the room and helped apply their fake fingerprints. In the end, no one would realize they had some type of glove on. The technology was impressive.

Finally, Tomas reached into his pocket and opened two small velvet boxes.

Wedding rings.

The final piece to their disguise.

"Give me your hand," he demanded.

Natalie extended her left arm.

The next moment, Tomas jammed the wedding ring on her finger.

He tossed the other ring to Joshua. "Put it on."

She stared at their hands a moment.

What would it be like if this was real? If she and Joshua were actually together?

And why did she have to keep thinking about him like this?

Maybe it was a welcome reprieve from her otherwise heavy thoughts.

Wasn't that what happened when people were faced with tragedy? Suddenly, other decisions in their life came into clarity.

Maybe that was happening now too.

If Natalie survived this . . . would she want to

stay in construction? Would she want to be a nomad forever and never get close to anyone again?

Or was there something more for her out there? Was the risk worth the cost?

She thought she knew the answer to that question as she glanced at Joshua.

"All right," Tomas said. "Let's go."

The next instant, Tomas's men pulled them from their chairs.

Then they stepped outside to begin what could be a deadly charade.

FORTY-TWO

APPREHENSION GREW inside Joshua as they left the shack where they'd been held and headed toward the vehicles.

He had a better look at the landscape now.

They were definitely still in the desert. The sun was just beginning to rise on the horizon, displaying the fact that they were surrounded by almost nothing.

The house they'd been in looked like it had been abandoned for years, as if it could fall down if the wind blew hard enough. But there was a fence behind it, and that's where all the cars had been parked.

No doubt Tomas and his men had done that so they wouldn't be discovered if anyone just happened to be driving past. Despite the state of disrepair, someone must own the property, and cars out front would be a dead giveaway that someone was using the place.

No doubt Tomas didn't care about trespassing.

He only cared about getting whatever he wanted.

Joshua had to keep a level head, go into that bank, convince the manager that he owned that safe deposit box, get whatever was inside, and get out.

As long as he knew that Natalie and Bella were safe, he would be okay.

But this was going to be a difficult situation. He couldn't show any nerves, or people would sense it.

Joshua was an experienced undercover agent, so he didn't think he'd have any problem. But he was worried about Natalie. Her fear showed all over her face.

He wanted to reach over and squeeze her hand. But he couldn't do that. Not now. Not where these men could witness the sign of affection.

Instead, they rode in the back of the SUV, surrounded by gunmen, as they headed toward Vegas.

He had no idea how far away it was, but he'd guess it was still a couple of hours away based on the sunrise. The sun rose at around 7:30 this time of year, give or take a few minutes, and banks usually opened at nine.

Upfront, the driver listened to Hank Williams and sang along. Tomas told him to shut up several times, but the driver kept singing about the Honky Tonk Blues.

The other gunmen grumbled as if they wished the guy would stop singing also.

But the driver didn't seem to care what they thought.

Finally, Joshua spotted the Vegas skyline in the distance.

He braced himself for whatever was about to happen next.

He and Natalie were going to need to put on the show of their lives.

———

Another rumble of nerves swept through Natalie. She had a feeling those wouldn't disappear until this was all over.

But she had to get herself under control now.

If anyone in the bank caught wind of how nervous she was, it would be a dead giveaway that she was lying.

And Bella would die.

Natalie would feel responsible—*if* she lived long enough to feel responsible.

She still wasn't sure what these guys would do with them when this whole operation was done.

They pulled into a parking garage beside the bank, and Tomas rattled off more instructions.

Then he held up his phone again and showed a live video of Bella. Just as before, she was still crying, still staring at the camera.

Joshua bristled beside her.

Natalie's heart squeezed at the sight of Bella's fear.

The poor woman . . . she didn't deserve this. None of them did.

"Remember, one wrong move, and she's a dead woman," Tomas said. "If you try to do anything—like escape—she's a dead woman. Don't think I don't mean that."

"We've got it," Joshua muttered, his muscles visibly tightening.

"Good." Tomas pushed a briefcase into Joshua's hands. "You'll need this for the contents of the safe deposit box. Now go."

Natalie's limbs trembled as she climbed out and steadied herself. Joshua met her behind the vehicle, a worried look in his eyes as he observed her. Then he frowned, took her hand, and led her out of the garage.

It wasn't until they could no longer see the Hummer that he spoke. "Are you okay?"

"As well as I can be, I suppose."

"What happened in that room? It sounded like he was hurting you."

"He wasn't. I . . . my bullet wound began to hurt. I let out a cry. Then I heard you struggling, and I didn't know what was happening to you."

He touched the knot at his temple. "I'm fine."

She frowned. He wasn't fine.

So much weight rested on his shoulders.

He was torn up inside over Bella. Worried about keeping Natalie alive. And had obviously been in an altercation with one of the guards.

They paused outside the bank, and Natalie turned toward him.

Her throat burned as she asked, "Are we going to be able to do this, Joshua?"

His jaw tightened. "We have no other choice. But, if this goes bad, I want you to run and don't look back."

JOSHUA PAUSED JUST outside the bank's front doors and leaned closer to Natalie. "Just take a few deep breaths."

She nodded quickly. Then she inhaled and exhaled as he'd instructed.

After doing so a few times, she turned back to him. "I'm ready."

He squeezed her hand harder as he stared deeply into her eyes. "I'm sorry you're in this situation."

"It's not your fault."

"It kind of is. This stuff comes with my job. But I don't like it when people I care about are pulled into the middle of it."

Yes, he had said it. People he cared about.

Natalie was definitely one of them.

"You care about me, huh?" she finally asked.

He pushed a hair behind her ear. "More than I was ready to admit. I can see how foolish that was now."

"Let's figure out how to get through this . . . then we can talk about us more. Okay?"

A small smile flickered across his face. "I'd like that."

She turned toward the bank and inhaled quickly once more before giving him an affirmative nod. "Let's just get this over with."

They stepped into the bank and approached the young, blonde clerk standing near the door.

"Good morning. What can I help you with?" she asked with a bright smile.

"We need to retrieve something from our safe deposit box." Joshua's voice sounded warm and even, with no signs of deception.

"Of course. Right this way."

She led them to a pristine desk where a balding black man sat. He looked up with a brief but affable smile. "Please, have a seat. I'm Deon. How can I help you?"

They seated themselves in front of him, and Joshua introduced himself and explained what he needed.

"Of course, Mr. and Mrs. Hollis. I just need to get some information from you first."

"Whatever you need." Joshua swallowed hard, knowing this was where it would all come together.

Or not.

Deon typed several things onto his computer before turning to them. "Let's start with some IDs."

Joshua and Natalie pulled out the fake driver's licenses Tomas had made for them. The counterfeits were surprisingly impressive, and Joshua was fairly certain that they were going to pass inspection.

Deon studied them a moment, and then glanced at them, and then looked at the computer screen.

Joshua held his breath as he waited for the man's response.

Finally, Deon smiled and nodded. "Very good, Mr. and Mrs. Hollis. We'll just need to verify your fingerprints, and then you'll be good to go."

This was it. This was the piece of the puzzle Joshua wasn't sure would work.

Deon pushed an electronic pad toward him. "Just place your fingers here."

Joshua swallowed hard before pressing his fingers onto the screen.

He was sweating.

He worried that the moisture could mess up the reading, mess with the fingerprint.

He held his breath as he waited to see what the computer would tell them.

When he saw the frown on Deon's face, Joshua knew something was wrong.

Deon looked up and shook his head. "Something must not be working right here. We're going to need to try this again."

Alarm shot through Joshua.

If they didn't successfully get the contents of this box, Bella would die.

Joshua would need to think of an alternate plan.

One that would keep everyone alive.

———

Natalie's heart beat so loudly in her ears that she could hardly think.

Why weren't the fingerprints working? Tomas had assured them they would.

She kept her expression neutral, trying not to show any signs of anxiety.

"Let's try again," Deon said.

As Joshua reached for the pad again, she cleared her throat. "I think you need to relax your hands a little bit more, darling. Based on my experience, these devices don't always work unless your fingers are placed exactly as they're supposed to be."

"That's correct." Deon nodded, not sounding

suspicious—not yet. "These things can be finicky sometimes."

Joshua flashed her a tight smile. "I'll try. It takes an effort for someone with a Type A personality to relax."

He placed his fingers on the screen again.

A sick feeling gurgled in Natalie's stomach as she waited.

She glanced at Deon's face, watching his expression for a sign of whether or not it was working.

Finally, he offered a subtle nod and smiled. "There we go."

The relief Natalie felt was only momentary.

"And now it's your turn, Mrs. Hollis. That's in our contract that both of you must be present."

"Of course." She felt the waxy tips on her fingers and prayed they didn't have any more snafus.

She sucked in a deep breath and exhaled, trying to relax herself.

Then she placed her hand on the pad and flashed Deon another friendly smile.

She waited, the seconds feeling like hours.

Beside her, Joshua squeezed her other hand.

The touch felt as natural as walking.

And it was a nice feeling.

Finally, Deon looked away from his computer. His

expression remained unreadable as he studied her face for a moment.

Natalie felt herself flush.

Was something wrong?

"It looks like you're both good to go." Deon seemed to relax in front of them. "I'll take you back there now."

Natalie's shoulders softened.

One obstacle down. Perhaps the biggest obstacle.

Now she and Joshua had to grab whatever was inside that safe deposit box and get out of there before something went wrong.

ONCE THEY WERE in the safe deposit room, the executive retrieved their box and set it on the table. He inserted his key into one of the two locks.

"Your key, sir?"

Joshua took out the key Tomas had given him and inserted it into the other lock.

They both turned the keys at the same time and the box unlatched.

Then Deon left to give them some privacy.

When he was gone, Joshua pocketed the key and turned to Natalie. "I can't believe we've gotten this far."

"Me either."

"Now let's figure out what's in this box."

Joshua held his breath as he opened it, anxious to

see exactly what was in it. What was so important that Tomas had to go through all this trouble.

To his surprise, it was a folder.

No jewelry. No cash. Just papers?

He and Natalie exchanged a glance.

Even though they'd been told not to look, there was no chance that was happening.

He opened the folder quickly, and his eyes widened when he saw the photos inside.

"Is that . . . ?" Natalie's voice caught.

"That's former President Bill Radar," Joshua finished, dumbfounded at the realization.

"Why do the Geminis have pictures of him meeting with different people?"

"That's a good question." Joshua quickly flipped through them.

Based on the way Radar looked, these weren't new photos. Radar appeared too young. They were several years old, if he had to guess. Based on the Secret Service detail around him, these could have been taken when he was in office.

"Do you recognize any of these people that he's talking with?" Natalie glanced at Joshua.

"I don't, but it seems as if maybe they were important."

When they finished flipping through the photos,

they saw several cassette tapes and a recorder at the bottom of the box.

"I know we don't have much time," Joshua said. "But I have to know what's on here."

"Then let's find out."

———

Natalie felt another tremble go through her as Joshua hit Play.

She'd known that whatever was in this box was serious.

And she'd say, based on these photos of President Radar, that she had been dead right.

A grainy recording filled the air as two men talked.

"No one can know about this," a deep voice said.

"Is this really necessary? There has to be another way . . ." The second voice was also male, but he sounded more anxious, his voice slightly high-pitched.

"There's not. We've looked into it."

"But innocent people will die . . ."

He fast-forwarded, and then heard the deep voice again. It clearly said, "The Overland Hotel."

Joshua clicked off the recording. He and Natalie exchanged a glance.

"Did I just hear what I think I heard?" Natalie asked.

Joshua nodded. "This is pretty much blackmail evidence against a former president."

"But for what? That's what doesn't make sense. He isn't president anymore."

"My gut feeling is that this has something to do with the terrorist bombing fifteen years ago in Florida that killed hundreds of people. It was at . . . the Overland Hotel."

CHAPTER
FORTY-FIVE

JOSHUA DIDN'T TELL Natalie what he was doing, but as she turned her back, he slipped one of the cassettes into his pocket.

It was risky. He hoped he didn't regret it.

But if this was what he thought it was, he needed a copy of it.

He had no doubt that Tomas would use this information to his advantage to take Radar down.

Maybe Radar *needed* to be taken down. That wasn't a question he was willing to deal with right now.

Right now, his and Natalie's time was running out, and they needed to get back out to the SUV.

Joshua placed the folder and cassettes with the recorder inside in the briefcase he'd been given then put the box back into the wall.

He plastered on a smile as they stepped back into the main area of the bank.

Was the executive eyeballing him?

He couldn't be sure.

But Joshua felt more certain than ever that he and Natalie needed to get out of there.

Now.

"Keep your steps steady," he whispered as he walked beside her.

But he felt her hand trembling in his.

As they reached the door, he thought they'd be scot-free.

But before they stepped outside, Deon yelled, "One moment! Stop right there."

Something was wrong, Joshua realized. Their cover had been blown.

Without a backward glance, he squeezed Natalie's hand tighter and took off in a run.

———

Natalie didn't know what Joshua was doing. Why didn't he just stop and talk to Deon?

There must be more to this.

Deon must have discovered they weren't who they said they were. That they weren't really Mr. and

Mrs. Ernest Hollis. Natalie heard the security guard on their heels, calling for them to stop.

How were they going to get to the parking garage without this guy catching them?

Then an alarm began to sound behind them, its wails pulling her nerves tighter and tighter.

Her heart beat harder.

What if someone tried to shoot them, thinking they were robbing the bank or something?

Things could turn ugly quickly.

Just then, Tomas's Hummer screeched to a stop in front of them. The door opened, and one of Tomas's men leaned out. "Get in!"

Just as a security guard gained on them, yelling for them to stop, she and Joshua jumped into the SUV. Tomas's men pulled them all the way in, then someone slammed the door as the vehicle squealed away.

Natalie's adrenaline continued to pump.

That had been close, and it wasn't over yet.

She glanced out the back window and saw the security guard staring after them, his radio to his mouth.

It would only be a matter of time before the police caught up to them.

Moving quickly, the driver, still playing Hank Williams, swerved onto the interstate. But now he was grinning, as if he enjoyed playing cat-and-mouse.

He veered off at the first exit and began to weave through a nearby housing development.

Where were the police?

Natalie had been certain the cops would find them.

But they hadn't.

Not yet.

The next instant, they pulled into a long driveway, then gates closed behind them, and two men ran out from an old house. They quickly switched the license plates on the vehicle. Added a Viva Las Vegas sticker to the window—she thought it said Viva Las Vegas—and they did something near the bumper. Maybe added a bumper sticker there also.

These guys were good.

They knew exactly what they were doing.

Natalie was sure that would not bode well for her and Joshua.

CHAPTER
FORTY-SIX

SEVERAL MINUTES LATER, they were back on the road.

Tomas's guys had successfully avoided the cops.

Joshua had to admit he was a little impressed.

Tomas turned toward them from the front seat and held out his hand. "The contents of the safe deposit box."

Joshua took them from the briefcase and handed them to the man.

Sweat trickled down his spine as Tomas began to go through each of the photos and as he glanced at the cassettes and the recorder.

"This is everything?" Tomas kept his head lowered, only glancing up with his eyes.

"Yes." Joshua could feel the pilfered cassette tape burning in his pocket. "That's everything."

"Very good. But you almost blew it."

"I'm not sure what happened," Joshua said. "Everything seemed to be going well until it was time for us to leave."

"Something clearly happened. You must've given yourselves away somehow."

"Does it matter now? We've held up to our end of the bargain," Joshua said. "Now you need to let Bella go. Natalie too."

"What about you?" Natalie's voice sounded tense with worry as she glanced at him.

Joshua didn't say anything. But he communicated plenty with his gaze.

He silently told her that this was the end of the road for him. There was no way he would walk away from this alive. Not after the way he betrayed the Geminis.

He lifted their joined hands and kissed the soft skin on the back of her hand.

Tears welled in her eyes.

"We'll let her go," Tomas said. "We just need to get you back to the cabin first."

"Why?" Joshua said. "You can let Natalie out here. You don't have to take her back."

Natalie squeezed his hand harder, almost as if refusing to let go.

"I'm the one calling the shots here," Tomas

snapped. "And I say we're taking her back."

Joshua fisted his free hand.

There was always a catch with Tomas. Joshua had seen it uncountable times with the Geminis. Diego—who'd been the leader in the past—always wanted just a little more.

It had always been just one more job. One more truckload of women. One more haul of drugs.

What would the "negotiation" be this time?

Part of him didn't even want to know.

But based on the smile on Tomas's face, this was far from being over.

———

Natalie's thoughts raced.

Of course, Tomas wasn't going to stay true to his word. Since when did criminals ever do that?

But if he didn't release them now, how would they ever get away?

She didn't know the answer to that question.

Most likely, they'd be found dead in that shack where they were being taken.

She shivered at the thought.

She glanced behind her one more time, halfway hoping to see a police car. She could wave frantically, get them to pull them over or make some type of intervention happen.

But there was no help in sight.

What exactly had happened back there at the bank? It didn't make any sense.

What gave them away? Why had Deon called after them?

Maybe it didn't matter at this point.

Soon—too soon—the city disappeared, and they headed into the desert again.

More dread seemed to gurgle in her stomach.

How were they going to survive this?

Even if they managed to take down these guys, they still didn't know where Bella was. They were still out in the middle of nowhere. And they were still both beat up and exhausted.

What exactly were these guys planning on doing with that information on President Radar? Clearly, they had big plans for it.

Natalie would bet that the former president would pay a lot of money to make sure those photos and recordings disappeared.

Which could mean he had something big to hide.

The truth churned at the back of her mind, but she was too exhausted to put anything together right now.

Joshua glanced at her and laced his fingers with hers.

Her heartbeat slowed ever so slightly.

She prayed he'd come up with a feasible plan.

Something that would get them out of this mess. Alive.

FORTY-SEVEN

WHEN THEY ARRIVED BACK at the shack, the sun stood high in the sky.

Seeing it again confirmed to Joshua that no one else was around for miles. The seclusion would not work to their advantage right now.

Tomas's men—there were four with them right now, plus the driver—led them from the car and shoved them toward the dilapidated structure.

Joshua couldn't take these guys out right now. They had too many weapons on them. Any sudden moves would only put Natalie at risk.

Instead, he led her inside.

As soon as he stepped into the room, he spotted Bella huddled against the wall.

When she saw him, she rose. "Joshua?"

Without any restraints, they closed the space

between each other, and Joshua pulled her into his arms.

"You're okay?" he whispered as he held her.

She nodded, but he could tell she was crying. "I'm so scared."

"I've been doing everything I could to find you."

"I know. I knew you would."

"Okay, enough with the sappy reunion," Tomas muttered beside him. "You three need to stay here awhile. I have some business to attend to, and then I'll be back to deal with you."

Joshua knew what that meant.

The man wanted to toy with them first.

To hurt them.

Then none of them were getting away from here in one piece.

Keeping an arm around Bella, Joshua watched as Tomas disappeared into a back room with two of his guards.

The two others remained in the living room area.

Was this going to be their only chance to get away?

It just might be.

But how?

———

Natalie glanced around the shack before leaning closer to Joshua and Bella. "Look at that support beam."

Joshua's gaze flickered toward the ceiling and the thick wooden beam running across the center of the space.

"What about it?" he asked quietly.

"It's buckling. And this post by the kitchen?" She used her eyes to show him where it was. "It's supporting that overhead beam."

"What are you getting at?"

"If we dislodge that post, this whole place is going to collapse with everyone inside."

"You mean, everyone but us?"

She nodded. "Exactly. I've seen a house like this before, one that we had to do demolition on. If we could figure out a way to knock down the post . . ."

Joshua glanced behind him before nodding. "I have an idea."

This was worth a shot.

He moved Bella closer to Natalie as he formulated a plan of action.

CHAPTER
FORTY-EIGHT

SUBTLY, Joshua edged toward the post that held up this side of the house.

Natalie and Bella eased along next to him.

There was an exit right behind them, and a guard lingered near it. But, if this place started to collapse, they could push past him and get out. One guard was easier to take out than four.

Joshua wasn't sure that this would be quite as easy as Natalie suggested, but it was worth a shot. They didn't have any weapons at their disposal, so they might as well make this house a weapon itself.

The idea was actually brilliant.

If it worked.

Casually, he leaned against the post.

As he did, he felt it budge a little.

Maybe this would be easier than he thought.

He glanced back at the guard by the exit. He wasn't paying attention.

The second guard stood on the opposite side of the room, blocking another exit.

The next instant, Joshua coughed. He coughed hard, bending over.

He made it seem as if he couldn't catch his breath as he had a coughing fit.

The two guards stared at him with narrowed eyes, almost as if wondering if he was up to something.

Natalie leaned over him. "Are you okay?"

"I'm . . ." He didn't finish as another cough claimed him.

The truth was that he was fine—other than the fact he was being held captive.

"Need some water or something, man?" one of the guards asked.

Joshua coughed some more before nodding.

"Please," he croaked out.

The guard lowered his gun as he went to grab a bottle. As he did, Joshua threw himself against the old refrigerator. The appliance tilted and started to fall, slamming into the post beside it.

The post held, but it creaked and groaned as it weakened.

The ceiling rocked above them.

Wood splintered from the post.

"What . . . ?" The guard looked up at him.

The beam overhead slipped a little.

The walls shifted.

Wasting no time, Joshua shoved the refrigerator into the post one more time.

———

"We've got to go!" Natalie yelled as the post gave way and the entire shack started to crumble.

Joshua took Bella's arm and led her toward the door. As he did, the guard with the water bottle stepped in front of them.

"What are you thinking?" the man growled.

"The whole place is going down!" Joshua told the guard. "Run!"

The dedicated man didn't budge.

Joshua shrugged. "Have it your way." He kicked the gun from the guard's hand before swinging his leg around and ramming the guy's face.

The guard fell to the floor.

As he did, Joshua threw the door open and yelled, "Run!"

Bella and Natalie lunged for safety.

Just as he followed them outside, a rumble sounded behind them.

The ceiling caved in, crushing the walls like an accordion.

Joshua pulled the ladies away from the flying debris as fast as he could.

They'd made it.

But they still had other issues right now they needed to deal with.

Like . . . how were they going to get safely away from here?

Dust flew around them, thick and blinding.

He needed to see.

Needed to find a car.

But he knew the basic direction of the Hummer.

He led the women that way.

He'd figure out how to deal with the driver once he got there.

As they reached the vehicle, the dust began to settle and a figure appeared in front of them.

Tomas.

He'd somehow gotten out.

And he had his gun trained on them.

FORTY-NINE

NATALIE SUCKED IN A BREATH, and immediately regretted it as residual dust filled her lungs. Instead of letting out a scream, she began to cough.

"That's not going to work again this time." Tomas stepped closer, still glowering at them. "You didn't think you were actually going to get away, did you?"

Joshua raised his hands. "You had to know I wouldn't go down without a fight."

Natalie noticed he kept both her and Bella behind him, putting himself in harm's way first.

She could admire that in a man.

"You betrayed the cartel." Tomas glared at him. "Nobody does that and lives to tell about it."

"You were hurting a lot of innocent people. I couldn't turn a blind eye."

"It's because of *you* that our organization has been weakened. But we're not destroyed. We will rise again!"

"So you are regrouping?"

Tomas's eyes narrowed even further. "You have no idea who you're messing with."

"You work for powerful people, don't you?" Joshua asked. "This goes beyond Miguel and Diego Sanchez, doesn't it? It goes beyond you. You're mixed up in something bigger."

"That is none of your business," Tomas snapped. "Let's just say we have big plans."

"I'm sure you do. But you haven't won this battle yet."

"We'll see about that." Tomas raised his gun.

A bullet fired.

And Natalie waited for the pain that would follow.

———

Joshua felt no pain.

He checked himself.

He saw no bullet holes.

Before he could glance behind him at the women, Tomas grasped his chest and fell to the ground.

"What . . . ?" Joshua muttered.

Where had that bullet come from?

As he glanced behind him, he spotted Bella. She held a gun in her hand, and a shocked expression on her face.

She must have grabbed the guard's gun as they ran out the door.

She'd saved their lives . . . but now she'd have to live with this burden.

"Let me take that from you," he murmured.

She was stiff with shock as Joshua took the gun from her hands. He handed the weapon to Natalie and then pulled his cousin into his arms.

She buried herself there. "I couldn't let him hurt anyone else . . ."

"I know, sweetie. I know."

As Joshua held her, he glanced back at Tomas one more time.

The man wasn't moving. But that didn't mean he was dead.

"We don't have time to stay here long," Joshua said. "We don't know who else will show up. We've got to get to that Hummer."

They all turned toward the vehicle.

As they did, the driver stepped out.

One look at the gun in Joshua's hand and Tomas bleeding on the ground, and he raised his hands in the air. Then he placed his keys on the ground and took a couple of steps back, turned and sprinted into the desert.

Joshua let the driver go. He had a feeling the guy wasn't an integral part of this organization.

Instead, he shouted, "Let's get out of here!"

They darted toward the vehicle. Joshua grabbed the keys from the ground on the way.

When the ladies were safely tucked inside, he cranked the engine, and they took off down the road, heading toward safety.

"I'M SO glad you all are okay," Charlie murmured to Natalie and Joshua as they stood outside the lodge two hours later.

Natalie was also glad everyone was okay. There had been moments when she'd doubted if they would survive.

The sheriff was here asking questions, and EMTs were looking after Bella. She'd have to be treated more later, but for now they were doing a quick examination.

Natalie wasn't sure what had happened to Bella during her time in captivity. The horrific details would probably come out over time.

Tomas and his men had been arrested. Somehow, they'd all made it out alive.

The driver had been captured and—in exchange

for leniency—had told police where Enrico's brother was being held. The man was going to be okay—but Enrico was facing murder charges and would be behind bars for a long time.

After Joshua, Bella, and Natalie had fled, they'd found the nearest town and had called the police. Then they'd continued back to the ranch.

Charlie had met them there with her crew, the sheriff and the ambulance waiting when they arrived.

It appeared Albright and Chester had nothing to do with this. Albright truly was in town on business, and Chester had fled simply out of fear. The sabotage had all been about the cartel, Joshua, and the ranch.

Natalie glanced around at the Vanishing Ranch crew that lingered close. Where was Monroe? Normally, wherever Charlie was, Monroe was also.

It was strange that he wasn't here, but maybe he was handling other business.

Regardless, Charlie didn't look as vivacious as usual.

Had Natalie missed something?

As Bella sobbed in the distance, Natalie's thoughts turned to her.

She glanced toward Bella and saw her emerge from the ambulance. Saw the tears streaming down her face—tears of both gratitude and trauma, if Natalie had to guess.

Joshua hurried toward Bella and slipped an arm around her shoulder.

She was trembling as she said, "This is Grundy's fault. He did this to me."

Charlie stepped closer, her frown deepening. "What do you mean?"

"He figured out I was trying to leave him, and he was furious. He beat me pretty bad. In fact, I could hardly get up off the floor. I didn't even try." She sucked in a shaky breath. "The next thing I knew, these men came and grabbed me. Grundy watched the whole thing happen. He looked happy about it. Said I'd finally be worth something."

Natalie reached over and squeezed her hand, sensing how horrible that moment must have been for her.

"I was thrown into the back of a van and injected with something."

"Probably heroin." Joshua grimaced.

"Everything is kind of a blur after that." She sniffled again. "I was taken to several locations. Other women were there. They all seemed the same as me —desperate, beaten down, doped up."

"You don't have to finish," Charlie told her.

That forlorn look filled Bella's gaze again. "The

good news is that I don't remember a lot of what happened. When they found out about my connection to Joshua, their primary goal was to use me as leverage. A lot of the women had it so much worse . . ."

"I feel like this is my fault." Joshua's voice cracked. "I'm so sorry, Bella."

She turned toward him. "It's not your fault, Joshua. I knew you were doing everything you could to help me. We need men like you out there to stop men like Tomas. This can't continue."

"We're doing everything we can to stop them and make things right." Charlie stepped closer. "Every person—everyone, even the forgotten—is important."

As another sob claimed Bella, Joshua pulled her into his arms and held her.

———

Once Bella was safely resting in the clinic at Vanishing Ranch, several team members met in the conference room. Charlie, Joshua, Natalie, Jesse, and Mateo were all present.

"I'm glad this turned out as well as it did." Charlie's voice didn't contain as much energy and confidence as it usually did.

Joshua realized one person was missing from this conversation.

"Where's Monroe?" He glanced around to make sure he wasn't missing something.

The shadows on Charlie's face grew deeper. "He was hurt when Tomas threw the grenade."

"What?" Natalie gasped and straightened in her seat. "Is he okay?"

Charlie swallowed hard. "He's in a medically induced coma in Phoenix. The shrapnel grazed an artery, and he lost a lot of blood. Plus, the shrapnel did some organ damage . . ."

Natalie reached across the table and squeezed Charlie's hand. "I'm so sorry."

Charlie's jaw tightened as if she fought to hold herself together. "Doctors are hopeful he'll be okay . . . but there are no guarantees."

Joshua didn't know exactly what Charlie and Monroe's relationship was, but the two seemed close. He could only imagine how hard this must be on her.

"Anyway, we almost caught up to you. At the bank." Charlie sucked in a deep breath as if pulling herself together. "We actually tapped into some of our connections, and your faces showed up on a security camera at the bank in Vegas. Our contact alerted us, but you were leaving the bank by the time we put the call in."

"That's why they tried to stop us," Natalie muttered.

"We tried to trace you from there but were unsuccessful."

"We had to pretend to be a couple named Mr. and Mrs. Ernest Hollis," Joshua said. "Does that name ring any bells?"

"I can't say it does, but we'll look into it." Charlie shifted. "Now . . . is there anything else I should know?"

"Actually, there is." Joshua reached into his pocket and set the cassette tape on the table. "I retrieved this from that safe deposit box."

Charlie's eyebrows shot up. "What is it?"

"I believe it's a recording of President Radar making a backroom deal with someone."

"What?" Charlie's voice lilted.

"There was a file with pictures as well," Joshua told her. "Tomas had them. I'm unsure if the authorities were able to retrieve them from the house or not. He survived the gunshot wound, but he'll be in the hospital awhile—before he goes to trial."

"I haven't heard anything about it. What exactly were those pictures of?"

"In the photos, Radar was meeting with various men," Joshua said. "I didn't recognize them, but I assume the photos were probably meant to be used for blackmail."

Charlie nodded as if thinking over the possibilities.

"There's one more thing you should know about the tapes," Joshua added.

"What's that?"

"The one we listened to . . . someone mentioned the Overland Hotel."

Charlie sucked in a breath. "Where the bombing happened. Where my grandmother was killed. The reason my father was most likely killed."

Joshua nodded grimly. "I knew you'd want to know."

She picked up the cassette tape. "Any idea what's on this one?"

He shook his head. "No. We only listened to a few minutes of one of the tapes."

"Does anyone know you have this?"

He shook his head. "They shouldn't."

She excused herself and then returned a few minutes later with a small tape recorder. She placed the cassette inside. A moment later, a grainy recording filled the air.

"No one can know about this," a deep voice said.

"Is this really necessary? There has to be another way."

"There's not. We've looked into it."

"But innocent people will die . . ."

"It's for the greater good."

"I just don't understand . . ." The second man's voice cracked.

"It's better if you don't."

A pause sounded.

Then, "So the Overland Hotel?"

"Yes, that's the one. We don't have much time to plan this. We need to move now if this is going to work."

As the recording ended, silence stretched through the air.

"President Radar was involved in that bombing . . ." Charlie murmured before running a hand through her hair. "This goes much higher than I ever anticipated."

"Than you anticipated?" Joshua asked.

"It's a long story." Charlie frowned again.

"Is this the evidence you need to finally bring down the people who killed your grandmother?" Jesse asked.

Charlie nodded, a new determination in her eyes. "It just might be."

As they continued to talk, Joshua and Natalie slipped away.

Joshua took her hand as he led her outside. No one else was around right now.

Good.

He wanted some time alone with her.

"Natalie . . ." he started as he searched her gaze and wondered where to begin.

Before he could, Natalie reached up on her tiptoes and pressed her lips into his. It only took him a moment to register what was happening. Then his arms wrapped around her, and he drew her closer.

Their kiss deepened—but only for a moment—before he pulled away.

"I was going to tell you how much I care about you," he started, keeping his arms around her waist.

Natalie grinned. "I know."

He grinned also. "You do?"

"Absolutely. You've shown that over the past couple of days. There's no doubt in my mind that you care."

His thoughts sobered. "I don't know exactly what the future holds. My job—"

"We'll figure that out in time."

Her words took him by surprise. "Why do you sound so certain?"

"Because you give priority to the things you value, and our priorities are already changing. We don't need to figure everything out right now."

"Maybe we could go on a date when all of this clears. We can talk more then."

Natalie grinned. "I'd like that."

"It's settled then. But in the meantime . . ." He leaned down for another kiss, giving her a glimpse of promises to come.

~~~

Thank you for reading *Narrow Escape*. If you enjoyed this book, please consider leaving a review.

Read Charlie's story in *Desperate Rescue*!

~~~

COMPLETE BOOK LIST

Squeaky Clean Mysteries:
#1 Hazardous Duty
#2 Suspicious Minds
#2.5 It Came Upon a Midnight Crime (novella)
#3 Organized Grime
#4 Dirty Deeds
#5 The Scum of All Fears
#6 To Love, Honor and Perish
#7 Mucky Streak
#8 Foul Play
#9 Broom & Gloom
#10 Dust and Obey
#11 Thrill Squeaker
#11.5 Swept Away (novella)
#12 Cunning Attractions
#13 Cold Case: Clean Getaway

#14 Cold Case: Clean Sweep

#15 Cold Case: Clean Break

#16 Cleans to an End

While You Were Sweeping, A Riley Thomas Spinoff

The Sierra Files:

#1 Pounced

#2 Hunted

#3 Pranced

#4 Rattled

The Gabby St. Claire Diaries (a Tween Mystery series):

The Curtain Call Caper

The Disappearing Dog Dilemma

The Bungled Bike Burglaries

The Worst Detective Ever

#1 Ready to Fumble

#2 Reign of Error

#3 Safety in Blunders

#4 Join the Flub

#5 Blooper Freak

#6 Flaw Abiding Citizen

#7 Gaffe Out Loud

#8 Joke and Dagger

#9 Wreck the Halls

#10 Glitch and Famous

Raven Remington

Relentless

Holly Anna Paladin Mysteries:

#1 Random Acts of Murder

#2 Random Acts of Deceit

#2.5 Random Acts of Scrooge

#3 Random Acts of Malice

#4 Random Acts of Greed

#5 Random Acts of Fraud

#6 Random Acts of Outrage

#7 Random Acts of Iniquity

Lantern Beach Mysteries

#1 Hidden Currents

#2 Flood Watch

#3 Storm Surge

#4 Dangerous Waters

#5 Perilous Riptide

#6 Deadly Undertow

Lantern Beach Romantic Suspense

Tides of Deception

Shadow of Intrigue

Storm of Doubt

Winds of Danger

Rains of Remorse

Torrents of Fear

Lantern Beach P.D.

On the Lookout

Attempt to Locate

First Degree Murder

Dead on Arrival

Plan of Action

Lantern Beach Escape

Afterglow (a novelette)

Lantern Beach Blackout

Dark Water

Safe Harbor

Ripple Effect

Rising Tide

Lantern Beach Guardians

Hide and Seek

Shock and Awe

Safe and Sound

Lantern Beach Blackout: The New Recruits

Rocco

Axel

Beckett

Gabe

Lantern Beach Mayday

Run Aground

Dead Reckoning

Tipping Point

Lantern Beach Blackout: Danger Rising

Brandon

Dylan

Maddox

Titus

Lantern Beach Christmas

Silent Night

Crime á la Mode

Dead Man's Float

Milkshake Up

Bomb Pop Threat

Banana Split Personalities

Beach Bound Books and Beans Mysteries

Bound by Murder

Bound by Disaster

Bound by Mystery

Bound by Trouble

Bound by Mayhem

Vanishing Ranch

Forgotten Secrets

Necessary Risk

Risky Ambition

Deadly Intent

Lethal Betrayal

High Stakes Deception

Fatal Vendetta

Troubled Tidings

The Sidekick's Survival Guide

The Art of Eavesdropping

The Perks of Meddling

The Exercise of Interfering

The Practice of Prying

The Skill of Snooping

The Craft of Being Covert

Saltwater Cowboys

Saltwater Cowboy

Breakwater Protector

Cape Corral Keeper

Seagrass Secrets
Driftwood Danger
Unwavering Security

Beach House Mysteries
The Cottage on Ghost Lane
The Inn on Hanging Hill
The House on Dagger Point

School of Hard Rocks Mysteries
The Treble with Murder
Crime Strikes a Chord
Tone Death

Carolina Moon Series
Home Before Dark
Gone By Dark
Wait Until Dark
Light the Dark
Taken By Dark

Suburban Sleuth Mysteries:
Death of the Couch Potato's Wife

Fog Lake Suspense:
Edge of Peril
Margin of Error

Brink of Danger
Line of Duty
Legacy of Lies
Secrets of Shame
Refuge of Redemption

Cape Thomas Series:
Dubiosity
Disillusioned
Distorted

Standalone Romantic Mystery:
The Good Girl

Suspense:
Imperfect
The Wrecking

Sweet Christmas Novella:
Home to Chestnut Grove

Standalone Romantic-Suspense:
Keeping Guard
The Last Target
Race Against Time
Ricochet
Key Witness

Lifeline

High-Stakes Holiday Reunion

Desperate Measures

Hidden Agenda

Mountain Hideaway

Dark Harbor

Shadow of Suspicion

The Baby Assignment

The Cradle Conspiracy

Trained to Defend

Mountain Survival

Dangerous Mountain Rescue

Nonfiction:

Characters in the Kitchen

Changed: True Stories of Finding God through Christian Music (out of print)

The Novel in Me: The Beginner's Guide to Writing and Publishing a Novel (out of print)

ABOUT THE AUTHOR

USA Today has called Christy Barritt's books "scary, funny, passionate, and quirky."

Christy writes both mystery and romantic suspense novels that are clean with underlying messages of faith. Her books have sold more than three million copies and have won the Daphne du Maurier Award for Excellence in Suspense and Mystery, have been twice nominated for the Romantic Times Reviewers' Choice Award, and have finaled for both a Carol Award and Foreword Magazine's Book of the Year.

She is married to her Prince Charming, a man who thinks she's hilarious—but only when she's not trying to be. Christy is a self-proclaimed klutz, an avid music lover who's known for spontaneously bursting into song, and a road trip aficionado.

When she's not working or spending time with her family, she enjoys singing, playing the guitar, and exploring small, unsuspecting towns where people have no idea how accident-prone she is.

Find Christy online at:
www.christybarritt.com
www.facebook.com/christybarritt
www.twitter.com/cbarritt

Sign up for Christy's newsletter to get information on all of her latest releases here: **www.christybarritt. com/newsletter-sign-up/**

www.ingramcontent.com/pod-product-compliance
Lightning Source LLC
Chambersburg PA
CBHW031439160726
47994CB00005B/1797